THE CHAIN OF CHANCE

While I was filling my toilet kit, I came across something solid. The automatic. It had completely slipped my mind. At that moment I would have liked nothing better than to ditch it under the bathtub; instead I buried it in the larger suitcase, under my shirts, then carefully dried off the skin around my chest and stood before the mirror to attach the sensors. There had been a time when my body used to show marks in these places, but they were gone now. To attach the first electrode I located my heart's apex beat between my ribs, but the other electrode refused to stick in the region of the clavicular fossa. I dried off the skin a second time and fixed some tape on either side, so the sensor wouldn't stick out beyond the collarbone. I was new at this game; I'd never had to do it on my own before. Next: shirt, pants, and suspenders. I'd started wearing suspenders after my return trip to earth. I was more comfortable that way, because I didn't have to keep reaching for my pants, which always felt as if they were on the verge of falling.

Stanislaw LEM

THE CHAIN OF CHANCE

Mandarin

A Mandarin Paperback

THE CHAIN OF CHANCE

Originally published in Polish as *Katar*
First published in Great Britain 1978
by Martin Secker & Warburg Limited
This Mandarin edition published 1990
by Mandarin Paperbacks
Michelin House, 81 Fulham Road, London SW3 6RB

Mandarin is an imprint of the Octopus Publishing Group

Copyright © 1975 by Stanislaw Lem
English translation copyright © 1978 by Stanislaw Lem

A CIP catalogue record for this book
is available from the British Library
ISBN 0 7493 0489 8

Printed and bound in Great Britain
by Cox and Wyman Limited, Reading, Berks.

THE CHAIN
OF
CHANCE

Naples–Rome

The last day was by far the longest and most drawn out. Not that I was nervous or scared; I had no reason to be. Surrounded by a multilingual crowd, I felt lonely the whole time. No one took any notice of me; even my escorts kept out of sight. Besides, they were total strangers to me. I should actually have felt relieved knowing that by tomorrow I would be shedding my false skin, because not for a moment did I believe I was tempting fate by sleeping in Adams's pajamas, shaving with his razor, and retracing his steps around the bay. Nor was I expecting an ambush along the way—not the slightest harm had come to him on the highway—and during my one night in Rome I was to be given special protection. I was just anxious to get it over with, I told myself, now that the mission had proved a failure anyway. I told myself a lot of other sensible things, but that didn't stop me from continually upsetting my daily schedule.

After a trip to the baths I was scheduled to be back at the Vesuvio by three o'clock. But at twenty past two I was already heading toward the hotel as if hounded there by something. There was no chance of anything's happening in my room, so I walked up and down the street for a while. I knew the neighborhood inside out—the barbershop on the corner, the tobacconist's a few doors down, the travel agency, followed by the hotel parking lot set back in a row of houses. If you walked uphill past the hotel, you passed the boot shop where Adams had left the suitcase with the broken handle for repair—and a small, round-the-clock movie house. The first evening I almost ducked inside, after mistaking the rosy-pink spheres on the posters for planets. Not until I was standing in front of the box office did I notice my mistake: displayed on the poster was an enormous fanny. The stagnant heat was starting to get to me, so I hurried back to the corner and turned, to find a street vendor peddling his almonds—last year's supply of chestnuts had already run out. After scanning the selection of pipes in the window, I stepped into the tobacconist's and bought a pack of Kools, even though I was not in the habit of smoking menthols. The hoarse guttural sounds from the movie loudspeakers carried above the noisy traffic, reminding me of a slaughterhouse. Meanwhile the almond vendor had pushed his cart into the shade of the Vesuvio's sheltered driveway.

Everything testified to the gradual decline of what must have been an elegant hotel at one time. The lobby was practically deserted, and the inside of the elevator was cooler than my room. I scrutinized my surroundings. Packing in this heat would mean working up a good sweat, in which case the sensors wouldn't stick. I decided to pack in the bathroom, which in this old hotel was nearly as big as my room. The air in the bathroom was just as stuffy, but at least there was a marble floor. I took a shower in a tub supported by lions' paws; then, without drying off completely, standing barefoot to savor the coolness beneath my feet, I began stuffing things into my suitcases. While I was filling my toilet kit, I came across something solid. The automatic. It had completely slipped my mind. At that moment I would have liked nothing better than to ditch it under the bathtub; instead I buried it in the larger suitcase, under my shirts, then carefully dried off the skin around my chest and stood before the mirror to attach the sensors. There had been a time when my body used to show marks in these places, but they were gone now. To attach the first electrode I located my heart's apex beat between my ribs, but the other electrode refused to stick in the region of the clavicular fossa. I dried off the skin a second time and fixed some tape on either side, so the sensor wouldn't stick out beyond the collarbone. I was new at this game; I'd never had to do it on my own before. Next: shirt, pants, and suspenders. I'd started wearing suspenders after my return trip to earth. I was more comfortable that way, because I didn't have to keep reaching for my pants, which always felt as if they were on the verge of falling. When you're in orbit your clothes are weightless, but as soon as you're back on earth the "trouser reflex" sets in; hence the suspenders.

I was ready. I had the whole plan down pat. Three-quarters of an hour for lunch, taking care of the bill, and picking up the car keys; a half hour to reach the highway, which allowed for rush-hour traffic with ten minutes to spare. I checked the chest of drawers, set my luggage down by the door, splashed some cold water on my face, made a final inspection in the mirror to make sure the sensors weren't visible, and took the elevator downstairs. The restaurant was already packed. A waiter dripping with sweat set a bottle of chianti down in front of me, and I ordered a spaghetti dish with a basil sauce, and a Thermos of coffee. I'd just finished my meal and was checking the time when a garbled message came over the loudspeaker: "Telephone call for Mr. Adams!" I watched as the tiny bristles lining the back of my hands stood on end. Should I go to the phone, or shouldn't I? A barrel-bellied man in a peacock-blue shirt got up from a small table by the window and headed for the telephone booth. Somebody else with the same name. Adams was certainly a common enough name. I realized now it was a false alarm, but I was still annoyed with myself: it turned out my composure was only skin deep. I wiped my mouth to get rid of the olive oil, swallowed a bitter-tasting pill, washed it down with the rest of the wine, and got up to go to the reception desk. The hotel still prided itself on its plush furniture, stucco ornaments, and velvet coverings, though it wasn't hard to detect various kitchen odors coming from the back. The hotel: an aristocrat belching with sauerkraut.

That was the extent of my farewell. A porter carried out my bags, and I followed him into the stubborn heat. A Hertz rental car was waiting, with two wheels rolled up onto the curb. A Hornet, black as a hearse. I stopped the porter just in time from loading my luggage into the trunk, where I had a hunch the transmitter was stored, and sent him on his way with a tip. Climbing into the car was like climbing into an oven. I immediately broke out in a sweat and reached into my pocket for the gloves. Unnecessary, since the steering wheel was upholstered with leather. The trunk turned out to be empty—so where could they have put the amplifier? It was lying on the floorboard on the passenger's side, hidden underneath a magazine that was spread out in such a way that a naked blonde on the cover lay staring up at me passively, with her moist and shiny tongue hanging out. I made no sound, but something inside me quietly groaned as I began merging with the heavy traffic. A solid line from one light to the next. Even though I'd slept enough, I felt moody and on edge, first grouchy and then a little giddy. That's what I got for eating all that damned spaghetti, which I normally couldn't stand. It was always the same: the greater the danger, the more weight I'd put on. At the next intersection I turned on the blower, which immediately began bubbling with exhaust fumes. I switched it off. Cars were lined up bumper to bumper, Italian style. A detour. In both mirrors nothing but car roofs and automobile hoods, *la potente benzina italiana* stank of carbon monoxide, and I was stalled behind a bus, trapped in its smelly exhaust fumes. Some kids, all wearing the same green caps, sat gawking at me through the rear window. My stomach felt like a lump of dough, my head was on fire, and stuck to my heart was a sensor that caught on my suspenders every time I turned the wheel. I broke open a package of Kleenex and stuck a few tissues on top of the steering column. My nose was starting to tickle the way it always did before a storm. I sneezed once, twice, and soon was so busy sneezing I lost track of ever having left Naples, now fading in the azure coastal sky. I was cruising along the Strada del Sole now. Traffic was pretty light for the rush hour, but it was as if I'd never taken the Plimasine: my eyes were tingling and my nose was running, though my mouth was dry. I could have used some coffee, though I'd already drunk two cappuccinos back at the hotel, but the first coffee break wasn't till Magdalena. *The Herald* wasn't on the stands again because of some strike or other. While I was boxed in between some smoking Fiats and a Mercedes, I turned on the radio. It was a news broadcast, though most of it was lost on me. Some demonstrators had set fire to a building. One of the security guards was interviewed. The feminist underground promised more demonstrations in the future; then a woman, speaking in a deep alto, read a proclamation by the terrorists condemning the Pope, followed by various voices of the press. . . .

A women's underground. Nothing took one by surprise any more. People had lost all capacity to be surprised. What were they fighting against, anyhow? The tyranny of men? I didn't feel like a tyrant, any more than others did. Woe to the playboys! What were they planning to do to them? Would they wind up kidnapping the clergy, too? I shut off the radio as if slamming shut a garbage chute.

To have been in Naples and not seen Vesuvius—it was almost unforgivable of me. All the more so since I'd always been amiably disposed toward volcanoes. Half a century ago my father used to tell me bedtime stories about them. I'm turning into an old man, I thought, and was as stunned by this last thought as if I'd said I was on the verge of becoming a cow. Volcanoes were something solid, something that inspired trust. The earth erupts, lava spills, houses collapse. Everything looks so marvelous and simple to a five-year-old. I was sure you could reach the center of the earth by climbing down a crater, though my father had disputed that. Too bad he died when he did; he'd have been so proud of me. You don't have time to contemplate the terrifying silence of those infinite expanses when you're listening to the marvelous sound of the couplers as they moor the space vehicle to the module. Granted, my career had been a short one, and all because I'd proved myself unworthy of Mars. He'd have taken the news a lot harder than I did. What the hell—would you rather have had him die right after your first flight, so he could have closed his eyes still believing in you? Now, was that cynical or just plain petty of me? Better keep your eyes on the road.

As I was squeezing in behind a psychedelic-painted Lancia, I glanced in the mirror. Not a sign of the Hertz-rented Chrysler. Something had flashed back in the vicinity of Marianelli, but I couldn't be sure, because the other car had dropped out of sight again. On me alone did this short and monotonous highway, now teeming with an energetic mob on wheels, bestow the privilege of its secret, a secret that had uncannily eluded the police of both the old and new worlds combined. I alone had in my car trunk an air mattress, a surfboard, and a badminton racket intended not for sport and recreation but for inviting a treacherous blow from out of the unknown. I tried to get a little worked up, but the whole affair had ceased to be an adventure, had lost its charm. My thoughts were no longer on the mystery of the deadly conspiracy, only on whether it was time for another Plimasine to stop my constantly runny nose. I didn't care any more where the Chrysler was; besides, the transmitter had a hundred-mile range. My grandmother once had had a pair of bloomers on the attic line matching the color of that Lancia.

At six-twenty I began stepping on the gas. For a while I stayed behind a Volkswagen with a pair of sheep's eyes painted on the back that kept staring at me in tender reproach. The car is an amplifier of the personality. Later I cut in behind a fellow countryman from Arizona with a bumper sticker that read: HAVE A NICE DAY. In front and in back of me were cars piled high with outboards, water skis, golf bags, fishing gear, paddle boards, and bundles in all shapes and colors including orange and raspberry-red: Europe was doing its damnedest to "have a nice day." I held up my right hand and then my left one, as I'd done so many times in the past, and examined my outstretched fingers. Not one of them was shaking. They say that's the first sign. But who's to say for sure? No one can claim to be an authority in such matters. If I held my breath for a whole minute, Randy would certainly panic. What a half-assed idea!

A viaduct. The air made a flapping noise along the concrete uprights. I stole a glance at the scenery, a marvelous panorama of desolate green stretching all the way to the mountains that framed the horizon. A Ferrari as flat as a bedbug chased me out of the fast lane, and I broke out in another fit of sneezing that sounded more like swearing. My windshield was dotted with the remains of flies, my pant legs were sticking to my calves, and the glare from the wipers was killing my eyes. As I went to blow my nose, the package of Kleenex slipped down into the gap between the front seats and made a rustling noise. Who can describe that still-life spectacle that takes place in orbit? Just when you think you've got everything tied, secured, magnetized, and taped down with adhesive, the real show begins—that whirling swarm of felt-tip pencils, eyeglasses, and the loose ends of cables writhing about in space like lizards. Worst of all were the crumbs, hunting for crumbs with a vacuum cleaner. . . .

Or dandruff. The hidden background of mankind's cosmic steps was usually passed over in silence. Only children would dare to ask how you pee on the moon.

The mountains loomed up brown and sturdy, serene and somehow familiar. One of earth's more scenic spots. When the road later changed direction, the sun started shifting around the car's interior in a rectangular pattern, reminding me of the silent and majestic rotation of light inside the cabin. Day lurking within night, the one merging with the other as before the creation of the world, and then man's dream of flying becomes a reality, and the body's confusion, its dismay when the impossible becomes possible . . .

Although I'd attended a number of lectures on motion sickness, I had my own thoughts on the subject. Motion sickness was no ordinary attack of nausea, but a panic of the intestines and the spleen; though not usually conspicuous, they protested. Their bewilderment evoked only pity in me. All the time we were enjoying the cosmos, it was making them sick. They couldn't take it from the start. When we insisted on dragging them there, they revolted, though training obviously helped. But even if a bear can be taught to ride a bicycle, that doesn't mean he's cut out for it. The whole thing was ridiculous. We kept at it till the cerebral congestion and hardening of the intestines went away, but that was only postponing the inevitable: sooner or later we had to come back down. After landing on earth we had to put up with the excruciating pressure, the painful ordeal of having to unbend our knees and backs, and the sensation of having our heads spin around like bullets. I was fully aware of the effects, because I'd often seen athletically trained men made so uncomfortable by their inability to move that they would have to be lowered into tubs where they could be momentarily freed of bodily weight. Damned if I know what made me think it'd be any different with me.

According to that bearded psychologist, my own case was not exceptional. But even after you regained your sense of gravity, the experience of orbital weightlessness would come back to haunt you as a kind of nostalgia. We're not meant for the cosmos, and for that very reason we'll never give up.

A flashing red signal traveled straight to my foot, short-circuiting my brain. My tires made a crunching sound as they rolled over something like spilled rice, only bigger, like hailstones, which turned out to be glass. Traffic was slowing down to a crawl; the right lane was blocked off with traffic cones. I tried to get a glimpse beyond the line-up of cars and caught sight of a yellow helicopter in the process of making a slow landing in a field, the dust swirling under its fuselage like flour. On the ground lay two metal hulks, their hoods up and their front ends rammed into each other. But why so far off the road? And why were there no people around? Again the sound of glass crunching under tires as we drove at a snail's pace past a line of policemen waving us on with the words "Faster, faster!" Police helmets, ambulances, stretchers, an overturned car with one wheel still spinning and its directional signal still blinking . . . The highway was under a cloud of smoke. From burning asphalt? More likely gasoline. Cars began switching back to the right lane, and breathing became easier as soon as traffic started picking up speed. A death toll of forty had been predicted. Soon an elevated restaurant came into view. Next door the sparks of a welder's torch lit up the dark interior of the car repair shops located inside the sprawling *area di servizio*. Judging by my odometer, Cassino was the next exit. At the first bend in the road, my nose suddenly stopped tickling: the Plimasine had finally worked its way through the spaghetti.

Another curve. At one point I had the chilling sensation of being stared at from below, as if someone were lying on his back and watching my every move from underneath the car seat. The sun had fallen on the magazine cover featuring the blonde with the tongue on display. Without taking my eyes from the road I leaned forward and flipped the magazine over. For an astronaut you lead a pretty rich inner life—I was told by the psychologist after the Rorschach test. I couldn't remember which of us had started up the conversation, he or I. There were two kinds of anxiety, he claimed—one high, the other low, the first coming from the imagination, the second straight from the guts. Was he serious, or was he just trying to console me by implying I was too sensitive?

A hazy, washed-out film was all that was left of the clouds. Gradually a gas station drew near. I was just slowing down when some crazy old sport, his long hair blowing in the wind, raced ahead of me with a lot of racket and show in a broken-down Votan. I branched off toward the pumps, and while the tank was being filled I finished the rest of the Thermos, with its yellowish-brown residue of sugar at the bottom. No one bothered to wipe off the oil and blood spots on the window. After pulling up next to a construction site, I climbed out of the driver's seat and stretched my bones. Not far from where I was parked stood the glass-walled shopping pavilion where Adams had stopped to buy a deck of cards, imitation of Italian tarot cards dating from the eighteenth or nineteenth century. The station was in the process of being expanded; a mound of white, unlaid gravel stood surrounding a trench that had been dug out for a new gas pump. A glass door parted and I went inside the shop, which turned out to be deserted. Was it siesta time, I wondered? No, it was too late in the day for that. I wandered in and out of stacks of gaudy boxes and artificial fruit. A white escalator going to the second floor started moving whenever I came near it but stopped the moment I walked away. I saw a profile of myself on the television monitor installed near the front windows. The black-and-white picture flickered in the sunlight and made me look paler than usual. Not a clerk in sight. The shelves were piled high with cheap souvenirs and stacks of postcards all of the same variety. I reached into my pocket for some change. While looking around for a clerk, I heard the crunching of gravel under tires. A white Opel skidded to a halt, and out stepped a blonde in a pair of jeans who made her way around the ditches and into the shop. Though my back was turned, I could see her on the television monitor. She was standing perfectly still, only a dozen or so steps in back of me. From the counter I picked up a facsimile of an ancient woodcut showing a smoking Vesuvius towering above the bay. On the same counter were some cards featuring reproductions of Pompeian frescoes of the sort that would have shocked our fathers. The blonde took a few steps toward me as if trying to make up her mind whether I was a salesclerk. The escalator began moving without a sound, but the tiny figure in pants kept her distance.

I turned around and started for the exit. So far nothing out of the ordinary. She had a childlike face, a blank expression in the eyes, a delicate little mouth. Only once did I slow down while passing her; it was when she fixed me with those gaping eyes of hers, at the same time scratching the neck of her blouse with her fingernail; then she keeled over backward without uttering a sound or batting an eyelash. I was so unprepared for this reaction that before I could lunge toward her she slumped to the floor. Unable to catch her, I managed only to break her fall by grabbing hold of her bare arms as if helping her stretch out on her back of her own free will. She lay there, stiff as a doll. Anyone looking in from the outside would have thought I was kneeling beside an overturned dummy, several of which stood in the windows on either side of me, dressed in Neapolitan costumes. I grabbed her wrist; her pulse was weak but steady. Her teeth were partly showing, and the whites of her eyes were visible as if she were sleeping on her back with her eyelids half open. Less than a hundred meters away, cars were pulling up to the pumps, then wheeling around again and rejoining the steady stream of traffic roaring along the del Sole. Only two cars were parked out in front— mine and the girl's. Slowly I got up and gazed down at the figure stretched out on the floor. Her forearm, the one whose slender wrist I had just let go of, swung limply to one side; as it pulled the rest of the arm along with it and exposed the light-blond hairs lining her armpit, I noticed two tiny marks resembling scratches or a miniature tattoo. I had seen similar marks once before, on concentration-camp prisoners—runic signs of the SS. But these looked more like an ordinary birthmark. I had the urge to kneel down again but checked the impulse and headed for the exit instead. As if to emphasize the fact that the scene was over, the escalator suddenly came to a stop. On my way out I threw a final backward glance. A bunch of brightly colored balloons stood in the way, but I I could still see her prostrate body on the far television screen. The picture jiggled, but I could have sworn it was she who moved. I waited two or three seconds more, but nothing happened. The glass door obligingly let me pass; I jumped across the mounds, climbed into the Hornet, and backed up so I could make out the Opel's license plate. It was a German plate. A golf club was sticking up out of a motley pile of junk crammed into the back seat.

After merging with the traffic, I found I now had other thoughts to occupy me. The whole thing had the appearance of a quiet epileptic fit, *un petit mal*. Such attacks were not uncommon, even without convulsions. She might have felt the first symptoms coming on, decided to stop the car, then once inside the pavilion suddenly fainted. That would explain the blank stare and that insectlike movement of the fingers as she went to scratch the neck of her blouse. Then again, there was always the possibility of a simulation. I couldn't recall having seen her Opel along the way, but then I hadn't been that observant; besides, there was no telling how many Opels I'd come across with the same white finish and rectangular lines. I went over every detail in my mind, re-examining each as if through a magnifying glass. A shop like that must have had at least two if not three attendants on duty. Had they all gone out for a drink at the same time? Strange. Though nowadays even that was possible. Maybe they'd ducked out to a café, knowing that no customer would drop in at the pavilion at that time of day. And the girl must have thought it better to have the attack there, rather than at the station, where she had no intention of creating a scene for the benefit of those fellows in the Supercortemaggiori overalls. That all seemed logical enough, maybe even a bit too logical. She was traveling alone. Now what person in her condition would risk traveling alone? Even if she'd pulled out of it, I wouldn't have let her get behind the wheel again; I'd have advised her to leave the Opel parked where it was and to climb into my car. Anyone in my shoes

- 14 -

would have done the same. That's exactly what I would have done if I had been just a tourist.

The heat was beginning to get to me. I should have stayed behind and let myself fall into the trap—assuming it *was* a trap. That's what I was here for, damn it! The more convinced I became that her fainting spell had been real, the less sure I was of it. And not only where her fainting spell was concerned. People just don't leave a shopping pavilion unattended like that, not when it's nearly the size of a department store. At least there should have been a cashier behind the register. But even the cashier's desk had been empty. True, the inside of the store was clearly visible from the little café that stood facing it across the ditches. But who could have guessed that I would be going in there? No one. Anyway, it wasn't I they were after—unless I was singled out as an anonymous victim. If so, then whose victim? Unless they were all in on it together—the attendants, the cashier, the girl. But that struck me as being too far-fetched. A pure coincidence, then. So we were back where we'd started. Adams had driven all the way to Rome without incident. Alone, too. But what about the others? Suddenly I remembered the golf club in the Opel. Good Lord, those were the same kind of clubs that . . .

I was determined to get a firm grip on myself, even if I'd already made a fool of myself. Like a bad but stubborn actor, I went back to playing the role I'd flubbed so miserably. At the next gas station I asked for an inner tube without getting out of the car. A handsome, dark-haired man inspected my tires. "You're driving tubeless, sir." But I was adamant. While I paid for the tube, I kept one eye on the highway so I wouldn't miss the Chrysler. Not a sign of it. Fourteen kilometers down the road I replaced one of the good tires with the spare. I did it because Adams had made a tire change. As I crouched down beside the jack, the heat finally caught up with me. The jack needed oiling and squeaked. Overhead the sky was rent by the screeching roar of invisible jets, reminding me of the barrage of ship artillery covering the Normandy bridgehead. What made me think of that now? Later I had made another trip to Europe, this time as an official showpiece, as one of the crew from the Mars mission—though, as a backup pilot, only a second-rate, make-believe one. In those days Europe had shown me its more flattering side, whereas only now was I getting to know it if not better then at least more informally: the pissy back streets of Naples, the gruesome-looking prostitutes, even the hotel still boasting of its starlets but inwardly decayed and infested with street hustlers; the porno house, which once upon a time would have been unthinkable alongside such a shrine. But maybe it was the other way around. Maybe there was some truth to the rumor that Europe was rotting from above, from the top.

The metal paneling and tool kit were blazing hot. I cleaned my hands with some cleansing cream, wiped them dry with Kleenex, then climbed back into the car. At the last station I'd bought a bottle of Schweppes, but it took me a while to open it, because I couldn't lay my hands on the pocketknife with the bottle opener. As I swallowed the bitter liquid I thought of Randy, who was listening to me drink while driving along somewhere on the highway. The headrest was scorching hot from the sun's rays, and the back of my neck felt baked to a crisp. A metallic sheen lay shimmering on the asphalt near the horizon like a pool of water. Was that thunder in the distance? Sure enough, a thunderstorm. Most likely it was thundering that time the jets had roared across the sky, and the constant drone of the highway had drowned out the storm's fainter rumblings. Now everything was drowned out by the thunder, which cracked through the yellow-gold clouds till a pall of strident yellow hung over the mountains.

Some road signs announced the approach of Frosinone. Sweat was trickling down my back as if someone were running a feather between my shoulder blades. The storm, displaying all the theatricality of the Italians, rumbled menacingly without shedding a drop of rain, while gray tufts of cloud drifted across the landscape like an autumnal haze. Once, as I was starting around a winding curve, I could see where a long diagonal column was trying to pull a cloud down to the road. The sound of the first heavy drops splattering on the windshield was a welcome relief. Suddenly I was caught in a furious downpour.

By this time my windshield had become a battlefield. I waited a while before turning on the wipers. When the last of the insect debris had been washed away, I switched off the wipers and pulled over to the shoulder of the road, where I was supposed to stay parked for a full hour. The rain came in sheets and pounded on the roof, and the passing cars left blurry streaks of iridescent drops and billowing sprays of water in their tracks, while I just sat back and relaxed. Soon the water came trickling through the side vent onto my knee. I lit a cigarette, cupping it with my palm to keep it dry. The menthol left a bad taste in my mouth. A silver-colored Chrysler drove by, but the windshield was so flooded with water I couldn't be sure it was the right one. The sky was turning darker. First came the lightning, then peals of thunder cracking like sheet metal that was being ripped apart. To pass the time I counted the seconds between a bolt of lightning and a clap of thunder. The highway rumbled and roared; nothing could silence it. The hands on my watch showed it was past seven: it was time. I got out reluctantly. At first the cold rain shower was uncomfortable, but after a while it felt invigorating. All the time I pretended to be fixing the windshield wipers, I kept glancing out onto the road. No one seemed to take any notice of me; not one patrol car came my way. Soaked to my skin, I got back into the car and drove off.

Even though the storm was starting to ease up, it was getting darker by the moment. Past Frosinone the rain let up completely, the road was drier, and the puddles lying on either side of the road gave off a low white steam that mingled with the headlight beams. Finally, as if the land were eager to show itself in a new light just before nightfall, the sun came out from behind the clouds. With everything cast in an eerie pink glow, I drove the car into the parking lot of a Pavesi restaurant arching above the highway. After unsticking my shirt from my body to make the sensors less noticeable, I went upstairs. I hadn't noticed the Chrysler in the lot. Upstairs, people were babbling away in ten different languages and eating without so much as a glance at the cars shooting by down below like bowling balls. At some point, though I couldn't say exactly when, a sudden calm came over me, and I gave up worrying. It was as if the incident with the girl had taken place years ago. I relaxed over a couple of cups of coffee and a glass of Schweppes with lemon, and might have gone on relaxing if it hadn't dawned on me that the building was made of reinforced concrete: the interference might have made them lose track of my heartbeat. When you're transmitting between Houston and the moon, you don't have to worry about such problems. On my way out I washed my hands and face in the rest room, smoothed my hair in front of the mirror with a look of self-annoyance, then drove off again.

I still had some time to kill, so I drove as though the horse knew the way and all I had to do was to let up on the reins. I neither wandered in my thoughts nor passed the time daydreaming, but just switched off and pretended I wasn't there—"the vegetable life," I used to call it. Still, I must have been somewhat alert, because I managed to stop the car right on schedule. It was a good place to park, situated just below the summit of a gentle rise where the highway knifed through the top of the ridge like a perfect geometric incision. Through this slitlike opening I could see all the way to the horizon, where, with resolute energy, the asphalt strip cut straight across the next sloping hump. The one closest to me looked like a sighting notch, the one farthest like a rifle bead. Before cleaning the windshield I first had to open the trunk, because I'd already used up the last of the Kleenex. I touched the suitcase's soft bottom, where the weapon was resting peacefully. As though by some unconscious design, practically all the headlights went on at the same time. I scanned the broad expanse below. The route to Naples was streaked with patches of white that turned progressively redder as one approached Rome, where the road was now a bed of glowing coals. At the bottom of the grade, drivers were having to use their brakes, transforming that particular stretch into a vibrant strip of shimmering red—a pretty example of a stationary wave. If the road had been three times as wide, it could have been a road in Texas or Montana. Though standing only a few steps away from the edge of the road, I felt so alone I was overcome by a serene calm. People need grass every bit as much as goats do, and no one knows that better than the goats. As soon as I heard a helicopter churning through the invisible sky, I tossed my cigarette away and got into the car, whose warm interior still preserved traces of the afternoon heat.

Stark neon lights beyond the hills announced the approach of Rome. I still had some driving ahead of me, because my instructions were to circle the city first. The growing darkness obscured the faces of the people in the other cars, and the things piled high on the roofs took on weird and mysterious shapes. Everything was assuming a grave and impersonal aspect, full of hidden implications, as if matters of an extremely urgent nature were waiting at the road's end. Every backup astronaut has to be a little bit of a bastard, because something in him is always waiting for the regulars to slip up, and if not, then he's a stupid ass. I had to make another stop. The coffee in combination with the Plimasine, Schweppes, and ice water did the trick. I left the side of the road on foot and was struck by the surroundings. Not only the traffic but time along with it seemed to fade. Standing with my back to the highway, and despite the exhaust fumes, I could make out the scent of flowers in the gently fluttering breeze. What would I have done now if I were thirty? No sense brooding over such questions; better to button your fly and get behind the wheel again. The ignition key slipped between my fingers, and I fumbled around in the dark for it between the pedals, not wanting to switch on the interior light. As I drove along, I felt neither drowsy nor alert, neither edgy nor relaxed, but somehow strange, vulnerable, even a little astonished. The light from the lampposts streamed through the front windshield, turning my hands on the steering wheel white, then gradually retreated to the back of the car. Billboards came and went like phantoms, the concrete road joints drummed softly underneath. Now to the right, to pick up the city bypass that would bring me out onto the same northern route Adams had used to enter the city. He no longer meant anything to me now. He was just one case out of eleven. It was just a fluke that I'd inherited his things. Randy had insisted on it, and he was right: if you're going to do a job, then do it properly. The fact that I was using a dead man's shirts and luggage didn't faze me in the slightest, and if it was a little hard going at first, then it was only because these things belonged to a stranger, not because their owner was dead. While driving down a lonely and deserted stretch, I kept feeling that something was missing. The windows were rolled down, and the breeze brought the smell of flowers in bloom. Luckily the grasses had already retired for the night. Not once did I have the sniffles. They could talk all they liked about psychology; in the end it was the hay fever that had been the deciding factor. Of that I was sure, even though they'd tried to make me believe otherwise. What they'd said made sense, I suppose, because since when does grass grow on Mars? Besides, being allergic to dust is not a defect. Even so, somewhere in my files, in the space reserved for comments, they must have written the word "allergic"—in other words, defective. Because of that diagnosis I became a backup astronaut —a pencil sharpened with the best possible instruments so that in the end it couldn't be used to make a single dot. A backup Christopher Columbus, as it were.

I was being blinded now by a steady stream of oncoming traffic; I tried closing one eye and then the other. Had I taken the wrong route? I couldn't find a single exit. A mood of apathy came over me: I had no choice but to keep driving through the night. A towering billboard sign lit at an angle read ROMA TIBERINA. So I was headed in the right direction, after all. The closer I got to the downtown area, the more congested were the lights and traffic. Luckily all the hotels on my itinerary were located close to one another. At each of them I was greeted by the same gesture of outstretched hands— "The season! No vacancy!"—forcing me to get behind the wheel again. At the last hotel there was a vacancy, but I asked for a quiet room in one of the side wings. The porter gave me an inquisitive look; I shook my head with regret and walked back to the car.

The empty sidewalk in front of the Hilton was flooded with light. As I climbed out of the car I couldn't see the Chrysler anywhere, and it occurred to me that they might have had an accident, which would have explained why I hadn't seen them on the road. I routinely slammed the car door shut, and as I did I caught a glimpse of the Chrysler's front end in a fleeting reflection in the window. It was parked just outside the lot in the shadows, between the chains and a NO PARKING sign. On my way back into the hotel I could make out the car's dark interior, which looked to be deserted, though one of its windows was rolled down. When I came to within five paces of the car, the head of a cigarette lit up the interior. I felt an impulse to wave but resisted, giving my hand only a slight jerk before sticking it back into my pocket and entering the lobby.

This was just a minor incident, magnified by the fact that one chapter was over and another was beginning. The cold night air lent everything a marvelous clarity—the car trunks in the parking lot, the sound of my footsteps, the sidewalk markings— which made my inability to wave even more frustrating. Till now I'd stuck to my timetable as faithfully as a school kid, not giving a single thought to the guy who'd driven the same route before me, stopped off at the same places, taken the same number of coffee breaks, and made the same rounds of the hotels so that he could wind up here, at the Hilton, which he would never leave again alive. At that moment my assumed role struck me as something of a mockery, a willful defiance of fate.

A young punk, swaggering with self-importance, or perhaps only disguising his drowsiness, followed me out to the car, where he grabbed hold of the dusty suitcases with gloved hands while I smiled absently at his shiny buttons. The lobby was deserted. Another bruiser loaded my luggage into the elevator, which traveled upstairs to the sounds of piped music. I was still feeling the rhythm of the road, which, like a haunting tune, I couldn't shake off. The bellboy stopped, opened a set of double doors, switched on the wall light and overhead lamp, and turned on the living-room and bedroom lights; as soon as he was finished arranging my bags, I was alone again. Though Naples and Rome were no farther than a handshake away from each other, I felt tired, but it was a tiredness of a different kind, more tense, and that came as the next surprise. It was as if I'd polished off a can of beer in spoonfuls—a kind of stupefying sobriety. I made a tour of the rooms. The bed reached all the way to the floor, so there was no point in playing hide-and-seek. I opened all the closet doors, knowing ahead of time I wouldn't surprise any assassins because that would have been too easy, but I did my duty anyway. I lifted the sheets, the double mattress, and then the headrest, though I didn't seriously believe I'd never get up out of this bed again. Oh, yeah? Man is an undemocratic institution. His brain center, those voices from the right and the left, are nothing but a sham legislature, because there are also the catacombs, which bully him. The gospel according to Freud. I checked the air conditioner, then tested the blinds by raising and lowering them a few times. The room ceilings were plain and cheerful, unlike those at the Three Witches Inn, where the element of danger was so grimly conspicuous and where the bed canopy looked as if any moment it might collapse and smother you. Here there was no canopy, none of that syrupy, romantic atmosphere. Here everything—armchairs, desk, carpets—was neatly arranged in the usual display of comfort. Had I turned off the headlights?

The windows faced the other way, so I couldn't see the car. I was pretty sure I'd switched them off, and if not, well . . . let Hertz worry about it. I closed the curtains and started getting undressed, not caring where my shirt and pants landed. When I was completely stripped, I carefully detached the sensors. After taking a shower I'd have to stick them on again. I opened the larger suitcase, the one with the Band-Aid box lying on top, but I couldn't find the scissors. Standing in the middle of the room, I could feel a slight pressure in my head and the soft carpet pile beneath my feet. Then I remembered— I'd slipped them into my briefcase. Impatiently I yanked at the clasp, and out fell the scissors, along with a relic of the past—a photo of Sinus Aurorae, mounted in a Plexiglass frame and looking as yellow as the Sahara: landing site number I, the one I never made it to. On the carpet, next to my bare feet, it looked embarrassing, silly, full of nasty innuendo. I picked it up and studied it in the white light of the overhead lamp: ten degrees north latitude by fifty-two degrees east longitude, the patch of Bosporus Gemmatus at the top and the tropical formation below. The places I was to have reconnoitered on foot. I stood there with the photo in my hand, but instead of putting it back into my suitcase, I laid it down on the night-stand, next to the telephone, and went into the bathroom.

It was a jewel of a shower; the water came shooting out in a hundred hot streams. Civilization began with the invention of running water, with the lavatories of King Minos on Crete. For his tombstone one of the Pharaohs ordered a brick made of all the dirt that had been scraped from his skin over the period of a lifetime. And there has always been something vaguely symbolic about washing the body. When I was a teenager, if there was anything wrong with my car I used to put off washing it till after some work had been done to it, restoring its honor with a good wax job. For what could I have known then about the symbolic rites of purity and impurity and the fact that they had survived in all religions? In expensive apartments the only things I care about are the bathrooms. A persons feels only as good as his skin. In the full-length mirror I caught a glimpse of my soap-covered body still showing the imprint left by the electrode, almost as if I were back in Houston. My hips were still white from the swimming trunks. When I turned up the water, the pipes let out a mournful howl. The computation of turbulent flow that causes no resonances is still one of the seemingly unsolvable problems of hydraulics. What a lot of useless facts.

When I had finished drying off, not being too choosy which towel I used, I walked back into the bedroom stark naked, leaving a trail of wet footprints as I went. I taped on the heart electrode, but instead of lying down I sat on the edge of the bed and did some quick calculations: seven cups of coffee, counting what was in the Thermos. I never used to have any trouble going to sleep, but lately I'd acquired the habit of tossing from side to side. In one of my suitcases, unknown to Randy, I'd stashed some Seconal, a medicine prescribed for astronauts. Adams had never used the stuff, being apparently a sound sleeper. For me to take it now would have been an act of disloyalty. I'd forgotten to switch off the light in the bathroom. Though my bones were unwilling, I climbed out of bed. My hotel suite seemed to expand in the dark. Standing there naked, with my back to the bed, I hesitated. Oh, yes—I was supposed to lock the door and leave the key in the lock. Room 303. They'd even seen to it that I was given the same room number. So what the hell. I looked for some sign of fear in myself but was conscious only of something vague and undefined, of something bordering on shame. But I couldn't tell whether my anxiety came from the prospect of a sleepless night or from that of my own death. Everyone is superstitious, though not everyone is aware of it. I again surveyed my surroundings in the glare of the night light, only this time with genuine suspicion. My suitcases were half open, my clothes were scattered all over the armchairs. A real dress rehearsal.

Should I get out the automatic? Nonsense. I shook the self-pity out of my head, then lay down and turned off the night light, relaxing my muscles until my breathing became more regular.

Knowing how to fall asleep on schedule was an essential part of the mission. Especially when two people were sitting down below in a car and watching on an oscilloscope as a luminous white line recorded every move of my heart and lungs. If the door was locked from the inside and the windows hermetically sealed, what difference did it make if he'd gone to sleep in the same bed and at the same time?

There was a world of difference between the Hilton and the Three Witches Inn. I tried to picture my homecoming; I saw myself pulling up to the house unannounced, or better yet, parking the car by the drugstore and walking the rest of the way on foot, as if on my way back from a stroll. The boys would be home from school already; as soon as they saw me coming, the stairs would reverberate with their footsteps. It suddenly dawned on me that I was supposed to take another shot of gin. For a moment I lay there undecided, sitting up on one elbow. The bottle was still in the suitcase. I dragged myself out of bed, groped my way over to the table, located the flat bottle under my shirts, then filled the cap till the stuff started dripping down my fingers. While emptying the small metal tumbler, I again had the sensation of being an actor in an amateur play. A job's a job, I said by way of self-justification. As I walked back to the bed, my suntanned trunk, arms, and legs merged with the darkness, and my hips stood out like a white girdle. I lay down on the bed, the slug of gin gradually warming my stomach, and slammed my fist into the pillow: so this is what you've come to, you backup man! OK, pull up the covers and get some sleep.

Then I fell into the sort of drowse where the final flickerings of consciousness can be extinguished only by a state of total relaxation. A vision. I was sailing through space. Strangely enough, it was the same dream I'd had just before my trip to the orbital station. It was as if the stubborn catacombs of my mind refused to acknowledge any corrections dictated by experience. Flying in dreams is deceptive, because the body never really loses its normal sense of direction and the arms and legs can be manipulated as easily as in reality, though with greater facility. The real thing is another story. The muscles are thrown completely out of whack; if you try to push something away, you find yourself getting shoved backward; if you try to sit up straight, you find yourself tucking your knees under your chin. One careless move and you can knock yourself out. The body goes wild the moment it's liberated from earth's beneficial resistance.

I woke up with a choking sensation. Something soft but unyielding was interfering with my breathing. I bolted upright with my arms stretched out as if trying to grab the person who was choking me. Sitting up in bed, I tried to clear my mind, but it was like peeling some horribly sticky wrapper from my brain. A quicksilver glare from outside was streaming into the room through a crack between the curtains; in its shimmering brightness I saw that I was alone. I could hardly breathe any more: my nose felt cemented together, my mouth was caked, and my tongue was all dried up. I must have been snoring dreadfully. It was the snoring that had reached me toward the tail end, just as I was waking up.

I got up, still a little shaky on my feet because even though I was awake my dream kept weighing me down like motionless gravity. Carefully I bent over my suitcase, groping blindly in the side pocket for the elastic band holding the tube of Pyribenzamine in place. The blooming season had reached Rome. The spore capsules in the south are the first to turn reddish-brown, and then gradually the fading process spreads to higher regions, a fact well known to anyone who suffers from chronic hay fever. It was two in the morning. I was a little worried that my escorts might jump out of the car when they saw my heart playing funny tricks on the oscilloscope, so I lay down again and turned my head sideways on the pillow, this being the fastest way to relieve a congested nose. I lay there with one ear tuned to the corridor to make sure no unwanted help was on the way, but all was quiet. My heart resumed its normal rhythm again.

I gave up trying to picture the house. I was no longer in the mood for it, or maybe I realized it was wrong of me to drag the kids into this. A hell of a thing if you couldn't go to sleep without the help of the kids! The yoga would have to do, the kind adapted especially for astronauts by Dr. Sharp and his assistants. I knew it backward and forward like the Lord's Prayer. The exercises worked so well that before long my nose began to make a soft whistling sound as the passages opened up to let the air through, and the Pyribenzamine, once it lost its effect as a stimulant, trickled into my brain and induced its familiar but somehow impure sleepiness, so that before I knew it I was sound asleep.

Rome–Paris

At eight the next morning I went to see Randy. I was in a fairly decent mood, because I'd started the day with Plimasine and despite the dry heat my nose wasn't bothering me. Randy's hotel was nowhere near my hotel; it was located on a crowded back street paved in the Roman style, not far from the Spanish Steps. I'd forgotten the name of the street. While I waited for Randy in a narrow passageway containing lobby, reception desk, and coffee shop, I browsed through a copy of *The Herald* I'd picked up on the way to the hotel. I was interested in negotiations under way between Air France and the government, because I didn't relish the thought of being stranded at Orly. A strike had been declared by the airport's auxiliary crew, but Paris was still open to incoming flights.

It wasn't long before Randy showed up. Considering he'd been up most of the night he was in pretty good shape, except for being a little down in the mouth, but then by now it was obvious the mission had been a flop. Paris was our last resort, our last refuge. Randy offered to drive me to the airport, but I didn't let him; I thought it was better he got some sleep. He insisted it was impossible to sleep in his hotel room, so I followed him upstairs. As a matter of fact, his room was bright as day, and from the bathroom came the smell of hot suds instead of cool air.

Luckily we were in a high-pressure area. Relying on my professional knowledge, I drew the curtains, dampened them underneath to improve the air circulation, and left all the faucets running slightly. Having done my Samaritan duty, I said goodbye, promising to give him a call as soon as I came up with something concrete. I took a taxi out to the airport, stopping off at the Hilton for my things, and shortly before eleven was already pushing my luggage cart toward the departure area. It was my first trip to the new airport terminal in Rome, and I kept my eyes peeled for the wonders of its technical security system, which had been publicized in all the papers, never suspecting I would become something of an expert on it.

The press had greeted the opening of the new terminal as an event signaling the end of all terrorist attacks. The glassed-in departure area was the only thing that looked somehow familiar. Viewed from above, the building resembled a drum, traversed by a network of escalators and ramps that discreetly filtered the boarding passengers. Lately people had begun smuggling aboard weapons and explosives in parts, later assembling them in the airport toilets, which was why the Italians were the first to stop using magnetometers. The screening was now conducted by means of ultrasonic detection devices while the passengers were being transported on the escalators; the data obtained from this invisible search was then instantly evaluated by a computer programmed to identify smuggling suspects. It was reported that these ultrasonic waves were able to sense every tooth filling and suspender clasp, that not even a nonmetallic explosive could escape detection.

The new terminal was known unofficially as the Labyrinth. During a trial run lasting several weeks, intelligence experts armed with the most ingeniously concealed weapons had crammed the escalators, and not one of these smuggling attempts was known to have succeeded. The Labyrinth had been operating since April without any serious incidents; the only ones caught were those having in their possession objects as harmless as they were strange: a toy cap pistol, for example, or a metalized plastic replica of a gun. Some of the experts argued that such incidents amounted to a kind of psychological diversion on the part of frustrated terrorists, while others claimed they were merely meant to test the system's effectiveness. These pseudo smugglers posed something of a problem for the legal experts because, although their motives were unmistakable, they could not be considered punishable by law. So far the only serious incident had taken place on the day of my departure from Naples. An Asian passenger, after being detected by the sensors, had unloaded a live bomb on the Bridge of Sighs, which spanned the entire width of the Labyrinth. Hurled straight down into the hall, it caused an explosion that did little damage except to the nerves of the other passengers. In retrospect, I now believe these minor incidents were staged in preparation for an operation aimed at penetrating the new security system with a new type of offense.

My Alitalia flight was delayed an hour because of the uncertainty over whether we were to land at Orly or De Gaulle. Since the forecast was for thirty degrees Celsius in Paris, I decided to change clothes. I couldn't remember which suitcase I'd packed my summer shirts in, so I set out for the rest room with my luggage cart, which was too big for the escalator. I wandered in and out of the lower-level ramps until a rajah finally showed me the way—he was on his way to the rest room, too. I couldn't tell whether he was really a rajah, because although he wore a turban he had a very weak command of English. I was curious to see if he would take off his turban in the rest room. My little excursion with the cart had consumed so much time that I had to shower in a hurry and change quickly into my cotton summer suit and laced canvas sneakers. By sticking my toilet kit into a suitcase I was able to free my hands to make my way back to departures and to check in all my things as luggage. As it turned out this was a smart move, since I doubt whether the rolls of microfilm—they were stashed in the toilet kit—would have survived "the massacre of the steps."

The terminal's air-conditioning system was on the blink, blowing ice-cold air in some places and warm air in others. At the Paris gate it was warm, so I slung my jacket over my shoulder, which also turned out to be a lucky move. Each of us was handed an Ariadne Pass—a plastic pouch equipped with an electronic resonator—without which it was impossible to board any of the planes. On the other side of the turnstile was an escalator so narrow it could only be boarded single file. The ride was a little reminiscent of Tivoli and a little of Disneyland. The escalator climbed straight up till it gradually leveled off into a moving ramp that spanned the hall in a flood of fluorescent lights while the ground floor remained dark, though how they managed to achieve such a lighting effect was beyond me. Once past the Bridge of Sighs, the ramp swerved around and became an escalator again, cutting back at a steep angle across the same hall, which was now recognizable only by the openwork ceiling, as both sides of the ramp were lined with aluminum panels decorated with mythological scenes. I never did find out what the rest of it looked like. The idea was simple: any passenger having something suspicious in his possession was reported by means of an uninterrupted sound transmitted by the plastic pouch. The suspect had no possible escape, since the conveyor ramp was too narrow, and the constant repetition of passageways was designed to weaken him psychologically and force him to dispose of his weapon. The departure area was posted with signs in twenty different languages warning that anyone attempting to smuggle weapons or explosives aboard would place his own life in jeopardy if he tried to commit an act of terrorism against his fellow passengers. This cryptic warning was variously interpreted. There were even rumors that a team of sharpshooters was kept concealed behind the aluminum walls, but I didn't believe a word of it.

The flight had originally been a charter, but because the

Boeing made available turned out to be larger than the number of passengers, the remaining seats were sold over the counter. Those who eventually landed in trouble were those like myself who bought their tickets at the last minute. The Boeing had been rented by a bank consortium, though the people standing closest to me hardly looked like bankers. The first to step on the escalator was an elderly lady with a cane; then came a blond woman carrying a small dog, then myself, a little girl, and a Japanese. Glancing back down the stairs, I noticed that a couple of men had unfolded their newspapers. Since I was more in the mood for sightseeing, I tucked my *Herald* under the top of my suspenders like a fatigue cap.

The blonde, whose pearl-trimmed pants fit so snugly you could see the outline of her panties on her fanny, turned out to be carrying a stuffed animal; it was the way it blinked that made it seem alive. I was reminded of the blonde on the magazine cover who had accompanied me on my trip to Rome. In her white outfit and with her quick eyes, the little girl looked more like a doll. The Japanese, who wasn't much taller than the girl, was dressed to perfection and had all the mannerisms of an avid tourist. Crisscrossing the top of his buttoned-up checkered suit were the straps of a transistor radio, a pair of binoculars, and a powerful Nikon Six. While I happened to be looking around, he was in the process of opening the camera case to get a shot of the Labyrinth and the wonders of its interior. At the point where the stairs leveled off to form a ramp, I heard a shrill, drawn-out whistle; I spun around. It was coming from the direction of the Japanese. The little girl could be seen backing anxiously away from him, hugging her purse, which contained the ticket pouch. With a deadpan expression the Japanese turned up the volume on his radio, naïvely mistaken if he thought he could drown out the whistle: it was only the first warning.

We were gliding over the hall's vast interior. Looming up in the fluorescent light on either side of the bridge ramp were Romulus, Remus, and the she-wolf. By this time the whining noise coming from the ticket pouch of the Japanese had reached a piercing intensity. A tremor passed through the crowd, but no one dared to raise his voice. The only one who didn't bat an eyelash was the Japanese, who stood there expressionless, with only a few beads of sweat visible on his forehead. All of a sudden he yanked the pouch from his pocket and started wrestling with it like a madman, before a crowd of speechless onlookers—not a single woman cried out. As for me, I was only waiting to see how they would yank him out of the crowd. As the Bridge of Sighs came to an end and the ramp veered around a corner, the Japanese crouched down so suddenly and so low it looked as if he'd vanished from sight. It took me a while to realize what he was doing down there. Pulling the Nikon out of its case, he opened it just as the escalator was straightening out and beginning to climb again; it was now obvious that this second Bridge of Sighs was nothing more than an escalator moving back across the main hall at an angle. As soon as he was back on his feet again, there emerged from his Nikon a rounded, cylindrical object that glittered like a Christmas-tree ornament and that would barely have fit into the palm of my hand. A nonmetallic corundum grenade with a notched casing and no stem. The plastic pouch stopped whining. Using both hands, the Japanese pressed the bottom of the grenade to his mouth in the manner of a kiss; not until he removed it did I realize he'd pulled out the pin with his teeth and it was now sticking out between his lips. I made a dive for the grenade but only brushed it because the Japanese suddenly lunged backward with such force that he knocked those behind him off their feet and kicked me in the knee. My elbow landed in the girl's face; the impact sent me reeling against the railing. I banged into her again and this time took her with me as we both cleared the railing and went sailing through the air. Then something solid hit me in the back, and I passed from light into darkness.

I was expecting to land on sand. Though the papers hadn't mentioned explicitly what covered the floor, they were quite emphatic about the fact that no damage had resulted from the previous bomb explosion. Anticipating sand, I tried to get my legs into position while I was still in the air. But instead I encountered something soft and wet that gave way under me like foam until I landed in a freezing liquid. Simultaneously the blast of the explosion rocked my insides. I lost sight of the girl as my legs sank into some kind of sticky slime or mud; deeper and deeper I sank, fighting desperately with my hands, until a sudden calm took hold of me. I had about a minute, maybe a bit longer, to scramble out. First think—then act. It must have been a tank designed to soften the impact of a shock wave—a tank shaped more like a funnel than a bowl, spread with a layer of some sticky substance, filled with water, and then covered with a thick coating of an asphyxiating foam. There was no way I could charge uphill—I was knee-deep in the stuff—so I crouched down like a frog and began groping around on the bottom with my hands spread out; it was sloped to the right. Using the palms of my hands like shovels and pulling my feet out of the muck one at a time, I started crawling in that direction with all my strength. I kept it up, sometimes sliding back down the sloping incline and having to start all over again, using my hands to hoist myself up like a mountain climber trying to scale a snowy cliff without any handholds —but at least one can breathe in the snow.

I worked my way up high enough so that the big blistery bubbles on my face began to pop; half asphyxiated and gasping for air, I emerged into a shadowy penumbra filled with the concerted howls of those directly above me. With my head barely sticking out above the surface of tossing foam, I looked around. The girl was gone. I took a deep breath and dove below. I had to keep my eyes closed; something in the water made them burn like hell. Three times I surfaced and went below, getting noticeably weaker after each dive: since there was no way to bounce back up from the slime, I had to keep swimming over it to avoid being sucked under. Just when I'd given up hope, my hand accidentally touched her long hair.

The foam had left it slippery as a fish. While I was trying to tie a knot in her blouse as a grip, the blouse ripped.

How we made it to the surface again I'll never know. All I can remember is the frantic struggle, the huge bubbles I kept wiping from her face, the awful metallic taste of the water, how I kept swearing under my breath, and how I managed to shove her over the edge of the funnel—a thick, rubberlike embankment. When she was safely on the other side, I hung there for a while before getting out, standing up to my neck in the softly hissing foam and trying to get my breath while the howling continued in the background. I had the illusion that it was raining—a warm, fine sort of rain. I could even feel a few drops falling on me. You're hallucinating, I thought. Rain? In here? Arching back my head I caught sight of the bridge: aluminum sheets were dangling from it like rags, the floor was riddled like a sieve, and the stairs looked like a honeycomb cast in metal, deliberately perforated to filter the air blast and catch any flying debris.

I heaved myself up over the curved embankment in the gentle downpour and laid the girl face down across my knee. She was not as far gone as I thought, because she was starting to vomit. As I rhythmically massaged her back and sides, I could feel her laboring with all her little bones. She was still choking and gasping, but at least she was breathing normally again. I felt like vomiting, too, so I helped it along with my finger. Though it left me feeling better, I still didn't have the nerve to get up. For the first time I was able to make out where I was, though the poor visibility was made even worse by the blowout of a section of the fluorescent lighting. The howling overhead was giving way to sounds of groaning and gurgling. People are dying up there, I thought—why isn't anyone coming to their aid? There was a lot of racket nearby, mostly clanking, as if someone was trying to get the stalled escalator in service again. I could hear people crying out—healthy people, uninjured people. I couldn't figure out what was happening up there. The entire length of the escalator was jammed with people who had piled on top of one another out of panic. There was no way of reaching the dying without first removing those in a state of shock. Shoes and articles of clothing had become wedged between the steps. There was no access from the side: the bridge had turned out to be a trap.

Meanwhile I looked after myself and the girl. She was obviously conscious now and sitting up. I told her not to worry, that everything would be OK, that we'd be out of there in no time. And sure enough, once my eyes got accustomed to the dark it wasn't long before I spotted an exit: a hatchway that had inadvertently been left open. If it hadn't been for someone's negligence, we might have been stranded there like a couple of trapped mice. The hatchway opened up onto a sewer-like tunnel in which another hatchway, or, rather, a convex shield, also stood ajar. A corridor lined with recessed-light cages led us into a squat, bunkerlike basement full of cables, pipes, and plumbing installations.

"These pipes might lead to the rest rooms."

I turned to the girl, but she was gone.

"Hey ... where are you?" I yelled, at the same time scouting the entire length and width of the basement. I caught sight of her as she was running barefoot from one concrete pillar to another. Backache or no backache, I caught up with her in a couple of leaps, grabbed her by the hand, and said in a stern voice:

"What's the big idea, honey? You and I have to stick together, or we'll both get lost."

She tagged along after me in silence. It was starting to get brighter up ahead: a ramp flanked by white-tiled walls. We came out and found ourselves standing on a higher level. One glance at our surroundings and I knew where we were. A short distance away was the very same ramp I'd pushed my luggage cart down an hour ago. Around the corner was a corridor lined with doors. I took some change from my pocket, dropped a coin in the first door, and grabbed the little girl's hand on the hunch she was planning to run away again. She still looked

- 39 -

to be in a state of shock. Small wonder. I dragged her into the bathroom. She said nothing, and when I saw in the light how she was covered all over with blood I stopped talking, too: I knew now what the warm rain was. I must have looked a sight, too. After stripping both of us down, I dumped all our things into the tub, turned on the faucet, and, dressed only in my underwear, I shoved her under the shower. The hot water had a soothing effect on my backache and ran off our bodies in red streams. I rubbed her small back and sides. Not only to wash off the blood, but also to revive her. She submitted willingly, even passively, while I rinsed her hair as best I could.

When we came out of the shower, I asked her casually what her name was.

"Annabella."

"English?"

"French."

"From Paris?"

"No, from Clermont."

I switched to French, and started fishing our things out of the tub one by one to give them a rinse.

"If you feel up to it," I suggested, "would you mind rinsing out your dress?" She bent over the tub obediently.

While I was wringing out my pants and shirt, I contemplated our next move. By this time the airport would be shut down and crawling with police. So now what? Go merrily on our way till we got stopped somewhere? The Italian authorities weren't wise to my little game yet. The only other person in the know was du Bois Fenner, the embassy's first secretary. My airplane ticket was made out to a different name from the one on the hotel bill, and *it* was somewhere back in the hall along with my jacket. The automatic and the electrodes were still at the Hilton, all packaged and ready to be picked up by Randy that same evening. If they intercepted the package, I'd make a damned nice suspect, which I probably was anyway after making such a slick getaway and after going to such trouble to get rid of the blood. They might even accuse me of being an accomplice. No one was above suspicion, not since some respectable lawyers and a few other big shots had been caught in the act of smuggling bombs out of ideological sympathy. Eventually I'd be cleared of everything, but only after landing behind bars. Nothing like being helpless to get the police all excited. I gave Annabella a thorough inspection. A black eye, wet hair hanging down in strands, dress drying under the hand dryer; a bright kid. I started formulating a plan.

"Listen, honey," I said, "do you know who I am? An American astronaut, and I'm here incognito on a very important mission. Follow me? I've got to be in Paris by today at the latest, but if we stick around we'll be interrogated and that'll mean a delay. So I have to phone the embassy right away to get the first secretary to come down. He's going to help us. The airport's shut down, but there are other planes besides the normal ones, special planes they use for taking out the embassy mail. That's the kind we'll be flying on. You and me. Wouldn't you like that?"

She just stood there and stared. Not yet recovered, I thought. I started getting dressed. Thanks to the laces I still had my shoes, but Annabella had lost her sandals, though nowadays it was nothing to see girls running around barefoot in the street, and if worst came to worst her slip could pass for a blouse. I helped her straighten the pleats on her dress, now almost dry.

"Now we're going to play father and daughter," I said. "That way we won't have any trouble getting to a telephone. OK?"

She nodded, and off we went, hand in hand, to face the world. We ran into the first barricade the moment we stepped off the ramp. Some reporters armed with cameras were being forced back outside by the *carabinieri;* firemen, their helmets already on, were charging in the other direction. No one took any notice of us. One of the *carabinieri*—the one I happened to be talking to—could even get along in English. I fed him a story about how we'd been swimming, but without listening to a word I said, he told us to take escalator B upstairs to the European section, where all the passengers were being assembled. We started for the escalator, but the moment it blocked us from view I turned down a side corridor, leaving all the commotion behind. We entered a deserted waiting room where passengers came to claim their luggage. A row of telephone booths stood on the other side of some conveyor belts now moving quietly along. I took Annabella with me into one of the booths and dialed Randy's number. My call jolted him out of his sleep. Standing in a yellow glare, with my hand cupped around the receiver, I told him the whole story. He interrupted me only once, thinking possibly he'd misunderstood me. Then all I could hear was his heavy breathing, followed by a long pause as if he'd suddenly gone numb.

"Still there?" I asked when I was finished.

"Man!" he said. Then a second time: "Man!" Nothing else.

Then I came to the most critical part. He was to get Fenner from the embassy and drive down in the car with him right away. They'd have to make it fast; otherwise we'd be caught between two barricades. The airport would be shut down, but Fenner would find a way to get through. The girl would be right here with me. In the left wing of the building, next to luggage claim counter E10, right by the telephone booths. In case we weren't there, they could find us together with the other passengers in the European section, or else, for sure, in the custody of the police. I got him to recapitulate, then hung up, hoping the girl would acknowledge our success with a smile, or at least a look of relief, but she remained just as remote and tight-lipped as before. Several times I caught her spying on me, as if she were expecting something. An upholstered bench stood between the booths. We sat down. Through the plate-glass walls in the distance, the airport's approach ramps could be seen. Ambulance after ambulance kept pulling up in front; the continual racket of sirens and alarms was punctuated by women's spasmodic cries coming from inside the building. To make conversation I inquired about the girl's parents, about her trip, about who had brought her out to the airport. Her answers were evasive, monosyllabic; not even her Clermont address could I pry out of her. It was starting to get on my nerves. It was 1:40 by my watch. A half hour had gone by since my talk with Randy on the phone. Some guys dressed in overalls and wheeling what looked like an electric welding machine came trotting through the waiting room, but without so much as a glance in our direction. Again the sound of footsteps. A technician wearing earphones came in and started moving down the row of telephone booths, holding the little round plate attached to the mine detector up close to the doors as he went. He stopped in his tracks the moment he saw us. Two policemen closed in from behind till we were surrounded by all three.

"What are you doing here?"

"We're waiting."

I was telling the truth.

One of the *carabinieri* rushed off somewhere and came back a few minutes later accompanied by a tall man in civilian clothes. When I was asked the same question again, I replied that we were waiting for a representative from the American embassy. The plainclothesman asked to see my papers. As I was reaching for my wallet, the technician pointed to the booth adjacent to us. Its glass panels were fogged up on the inside— the steam left by our wet clothes. They were all eyes. The other *carabinieri* touched my pants.

"Wet!"

"Right!" I snapped back. "Sopping wet!"

They pointed their rifles at us.

"Don't worry," I whispered to Annabella.

The man in civilian clothes took a pair of handcuffs out of his pocket. Without wasting any time on formalities, he handcuffed me to himself while one of the other policemen looked after Annabella, who kept giving me a funny look. The plainclothesman had a walkie-talkie strapped over his shoulder; lifting it up close to his mouth, he said something in Italian, but so fast I couldn't catch a word of it. He seemed pleased with the reply. Then we were escorted through a side exit where three more *carabinieri* joined the procession. The escalator was still out of order. A generous flight of stairs brought us out into the departure area. On the way I caught a glimpse of the patrol cars lined up outside, and had just begun pondering our fate when a black Continental bearing the embassy banner pulled up in front. I can't remember when the sight of the Stars and Stripes has ever given me such a thrill. The scene that followed could only have happened on stage: just as we were making our way downstairs toward a glass door, du Bois, Randy, and one of the embassy interpreters entered the building. They were a strange sight—Randy in his Levis, the others in their dinner jackets. Randy started when he saw me and leaned over to Fenner, who turned to the interpreter, and it was he who approached us first.

Both groups halted, and a short, picturesque scene followed. The spokesman for the rescue team started up a conversation with the plainclothesman, the one I was chained to. The talking was done in a staccato manner; forgetting he was impeded by the handcuffs, my Italian escort kept yanking my hand up every time he made a gesture. I didn't understand a thing except "*astronauto americano*" and "*presto, presto!*" When my escort appeared satisfied, he again resorted to the portable radio. Even Fenner was granted the privilege of talking into it. Then the agent spoke a few more words into the set, which responded in a way that made him snap to attention; the situation was becoming more farcical by the moment. The cuffs were taken off, there was an about-face, and, falling into the same formation as before, only now with the roles completely reversed—those arrested were now acting as honorary escort— we headed upstairs to the first floor. On the way we passed a waiting room filled with passengers bivouacked on whatever was at hand, crossed a line of uniforms, filed through two leather-upholstered doors, and finally wound up in a crowded office.

With our arrival an apoplectic-looking giant started chasing people out the door. All but about ten people actually left the room. The hoarse, apoplectic-looking man turned out to be a deputy police chief. Someone offered me an armchair; Annabella was already seated. Despite the fact that it was broad daylight outside, all the lights in the room were on. Cross sections of the Labyrinth on the wall, a model of same on a portable stand next to the desk, glistening wet photos in the process of drying on the desk top. It wasn't hard to guess what was in the photos. Fenner, who was sitting behind me, gave my arm a slight squeeze: things had gone so well because he'd phoned the police chief directly from the embassy. There were a few people huddled around the desk, some others perched on the window sill, and the deputy police chief paced the floor in silent concentration. A teary-eyed secretary was ushered in from the next room. The interpreter kept shifting his head back and forth between me and the girl, ready to come to our rescue, but somehow my Italian improved significantly. I learned that my jacket, along with Annabella's purse, had been salvaged by a team of frogmen, thanks to which I was now a chief suspect, because in the meantime they'd already got in touch with the Hilton. I was suspected of being an accomplice of the Japanese. After releasing the grenade, we had planned to make a getaway toward the front, which was why we'd been among the first to board the escalator. But somehow there must have been a mixup in plans: the Japanese was killed in the explosion, while I saved myself by jumping over the bridge. On this point there was a difference of opinion. Some took Annabella to be a terrorist, others claimed I'd taken her as a hostage.

All this was passed on to me confidentially; they were still waiting for the arrival of the head of airport security before starting the interrogation. As soon as the latter had appeared, Randy, acting as self-appointed spokesman for the Americans, began briefing everyone on the nature of our mission. I listened, at the same time discreetly freeing my wet pant legs from my calves. He included in his report only what was absolutely necessary. Fenner was no less sparing in details, confirming that the embassy had been informed of our mission and that Interpol, which had also been briefed, was supposed to have notified the Italian authorities. This was a shrewd move on Fenner's part, because now the burden of responsibility had been shifted to an international organization. The Italians were not the least bit interested in our operation; they were much keener to know what had happened on the escalator. An engineer from the airport's staff said it was inconceivable that I could have escaped from either the tank or the hall without being familiar with the technical layout of the place. To which Randy replied that one shouldn't underestimate the sort of commando training administered by the USAF to people like me. He neglected to mention that my training days had been over thirty years ago. The sound of hammering vibrated through the walls. The rescue operation was still under way; they were cutting away a part of the bridge, the section torn apart by the explosion. So far they had dug out a total of nine bodies from the rubble, plus twenty-two wounded, seven of them critically. A commotion was heard outside the door; the deputy police chief motioned to one of his officers to investigate. As he was leaving the room I had a chance to observe, through a gap in the gathering, a little side table where my jacket was lying, with all the seams ripped open, and right beside it Annabella's purse, likewise demolished. The contents of her purse were neatly arranged, like stacks of poker chips, on little squares of white paper. The officer returned and, wringing his hands, said, "Newspaper reporters!" A few of the more enterprising reporters had managed to get this far before being turned back. Meanwhile another officer introduced himself to me.

"Lieutenant Canetti. What can you tell us about the explosive used? How was it smuggled in?"

"The camera had a false bottom. He opened it and the back popped out—film and all—like a jack-in-the-box. All he had to do then was to pull out the hand grenade."

"Are you familiar with this type of grenade?"

"I've come across something like it in the States. Part of the primer is located in the handle. As soon as I saw the handle was missing, I realized the primer was a modified one. A highly explosive antipersonnel bomb, metal content almost nil, with a casing made of solidified silicon carbide."

"And you just happened to be standing in that particular place on the escalator? Is that it?"

"Not quite."

I took advantage of the pause, a nerve-racking pause interrupted only by the hammering outside, to select my words carefully.

"It wasn't just by accident that I was standing there. The Japanese let the girl go ahead of him because he figured a kid would be the least likely to cramp his style. The girl"—I nodded in her direction—"was at the head of the line because she was intrigued by a stuffed dog. That's my impression, anyway. Am I right, Annabella?"

"Yes." She was visibly surprised.

I smiled at her.

"And as for me . . . I was in a hurry. It's irrational, I agree, but when you're in a hurry you automatically want to be the first to board the plane. And that goes for the boarding ramp as well. . . . It wasn't deliberate on my part, it just happened that way."

Everyone sighed. Canetti murmured something to the deputy police chief, who nodded.

"We would like to spare you, young lady . . . certain details of the inquiry. Would you mind stepping outside for a while?"

I glanced over at Annabella. A girlish smile—her first—just for me. She got up. Someone opened the door for her. As soon as she was out of the room, Canetti went at it again.

"Now for the next question. When did you begin to suspect the Japanese?"

"I never suspected him for a moment; he was so totally convincing in that tourist getup of his. Till the moment he crouched down, that is. At first I thought he was out of his mind. But as soon as I saw he'd triggered the grenade, I figured I had about three seconds, more or less."

"How many did you have exactly?"

"Hard to say. The grenade didn't explode right away when he pulled the pin, it must have had a delay mechanism. My guess is two, maybe two and a half seconds."

"That would coincide with our own estimate," said one of the men over by the window.

"You seem to have trouble walking. Were you injured?"

"Yes, but not by the explosion. The blast came just as I was landing in the water. How high up is the bridge? About five meters?"

"Four and a half."

"That would account for one second. My reaching for the grenade and clearing the railing would account for another. You asked if I was injured. I banged my back against something while I was in the air. I once fractured my tail bone."

"You hit a deflector," explained the man seated on the window sill. "A boom equipped with a diagonal shield designed to deflect an object into the center of the funnel. You've never heard of such a deflector?"

"No."

"I beg your pardon, but it's still my turn!" protested Canetti. "Did that man—that Japanese—actually throw the grenade?"

"No. He held on to it till the very end."

"Didn't he try to escape?"

"Nope."

"Poltrinelli, head of airport security." The newcomer was leaning against the desk, dressed in a pair of grease-stained overalls. "Are you absolutely sure the man wanted to die?"

"Did he *want* to die? Yes. He made no attempt to save his

own skin. He could have unloaded the whole camera if he'd wanted to."

"Excuse me, but this is an important point for us. Isn't it possible he planned to jump over the bridge after throwing the grenade but was prevented from doing so by your surprise attack?"

"Impossible. Though I could be wrong," I conceded. "For one thing, I didn't attack him. I was only trying to get the grenade out of his hands after he pulled it away from his face; I could see the pin sticking out between his teeth. It was made of nylon instead of metal. He was using both hands to hold the thing. That's not how you throw a hand grenade."

"How did you attack him? From above?"

"That's how I would have attacked if the stairs had been empty or if we'd been last in line. That's why he knew better than to stand at the back. Any hand grenade can be knocked loose by a straight jab from above, in which case it would just have gone sailing down the stairs. If I'd only poked it out of his hand, it would have landed close by. Even though it's against regulations, people still put their hand luggage on the steps. In which case the grenade wouldn't have rolled very far. That's why I swung from the left, and that's what took him by surprise."

"From the left, you say? Are you left-handed?"

"Yes. He wasn't expecting that. He ducked the wrong way. The guy was a real pro. He stuck out his elbow to guard from the right."

"Then what happened?"

"After that he kicked me in the knee and threw himself backward. He must have been extremely well trained; even if you're willing to die, it's hard as hell to throw yourself backward down a flight of stairs. Most of us would rather die facing forward."

"But the stairs were crowded."

"Right! And yet there was no one standing behind him. Everyone was trying to move back out of the way."

"He wasn't counting on that."

"I know, but nothing was left to chance. He was too slick, he had every move down pat."

The security chief squeezed the desk top till his knuckles turned white. He fired away with his questions as if conducting a cross-examination.

"I wish to emphasize that as far as we're concerned your behavior is beyond reproach. But I repeat: it is of vital importance to us that we get at the facts in this case. You understand why, don't you?"

"The question is whether they have people ready to face certain death."

"Precisely. That's why I must ask you to reconsider the exact sequence of events that took place during that one second. Let me put myself in his place. I release the safety catch. Next I plan to jump over the bridge. If I stick to my plan, you intercept the grenade and throw it back at me as I'm going down. I hesitate, and it's that split second of hesitation that proves decisive. Couldn't that have been the way it happened?"

"No. A person planning to throw a hand grenade doesn't hold it with both hands."

"But you shoved him as you were going for the grenade."

"No. If my fingers hadn't slipped I would've pulled him toward me. I couldn't get a grip on him; he got away from me by kneeling over backward. That was a deilberate move on his part. I confess I underestimated him. I should have just grabbed him and dumped him over the railing along with the grenade. That's what I would have done if I hadn't been so startled."

"He might have dropped the grenade by your feet."

"Then I'd have gone over the railing with him. Or tried to, at least. Of course it's easy to say afterward, but I think I would have gambled. I weighed twice as much as he did, and his arms were no bigger than a kid's."

"Thank you. No further questions."

"Scarron, engineer." The man introducing himself was young

looking but prematurely gray; he wore civilian clothes and a pair of horn-rimmed glasses. "Can you think of any security measures that might have prevented such an attack?"

"You're asking too much of me. It looks to me as if you've taken care of everything."

They were prepared for many things, he said, but not everything. They'd even found a way of counteracting the so-called Lod Type Operation. At the push of a button, isolated sections of the escalator could be converted into a sloping plane capable of depositing people in a water tank.

"One equipped with the same kind of foam?"

"No. That's an antidetonation tank designed strictly for under the bridge. No, I had other kinds in mind."

"Well, then . . . what was stopping you? Not that it would have mattered, really . . ."

"Exactly. His execution was too fast."

He pointed to the interior of the Labyrinth shown on the display map. The entire route was in fact conceived as a kind of firing zone, one that could be flooded from above with water released at a pressure great enough to sweep away everything in its path. The funnel was thought to be escape-proof; the failure to secure the escape hatches had been a serious oversight. He offered to take me over to the model, but I declined.

The engineer looked flustered. He was dying to show me the results of his farsightedness, even though he must have realized it was a waste of time. He had solicited my opinion hoping I wouldn't be able to offer any.

Just when I thought the interrogation was over, an elderly man sitting in the chair left vacant by Annabella raised his hand.

"Dr. Torcelli. I have only one question. Can you explain how you were able to save the girl?"

I gave it a moment's thought.

"It was a lucky coincidence, that's all. She was standing between us. To get at the Japanese I had to shove her out of the way; the impact of his fall made me collide with her. It was a low railing; if she'd been an adult I would never have got her over. I doubt whether I would've even attempted it."

"What if it had been a woman?"

"There *was* a woman," I said, meeting his gaze. "In front of me. A blonde in pearl-trimmed pants, the one with the stuffed dog. What ever happened to her?"

"She bled to death." The comment came from the head of security. "She had both legs torn off by the explosion."

There was a lapse in the conversation. Those seated on the window sill stood up, and there was a shuffling of chairs, but my thoughts kept going back to that moment on the escalator. One thing I knew: I hadn't wasted any time in going over the railing. Grabbing hold of it with my right arm, I'd taken off from the step with my other arm wrapped around the girl. By hurdling the railing in the manner of a side vault, I'd forced her to accompany me on my way down. Whether I'd put my arm around her deliberately or because she just happened to be standing there, I couldn't say.

Although they were through with me, I wanted some assurance I would be spared any publicity. This was interpreted as an expression of undue modesty, something I refused to admit. It had nothing to do with modesty. I simply had no desire to become personally implicated in the "massacre on the steps." The only one who guessed my real motive was Randy.

Fenner suggested I stay overnight in Rome as a guest of the embassy. But on this point I was equally adamant: I insisted on taking the next available flight to Paris, which turned out to be a Cessna carrying a shipment of materials used at a conference that had ended that afternoon with a cocktail reception; this explained why Fenner and the interpreter had arrived in dinner jackets. We were drifting toward the door in small groups, still engaged in conversation, when a woman with magnificent dark eyes, whose presence I had overlooked till now, took me aside. She turned out to be a psychologist, the one who'd been looking after Annabella. She asked if I was serious about wanting to take the girl along with me to Paris.

"Why, yes. She must have told you about my promise."

A smile. She asked whether I had any children of my own.

"No. Well . . . let's say not quite. I have two nephews."

"And are they very fond of you?"

"You bet they are."

She then revealed Annabella's secret. The girl had been worried sick. Even though I'd saved her life she had a very low opinion of me, taking me for an accomplice of the Japanese or something very close to it. That's why she'd tried to run away. In the rest room I gave her an even worse scare.

"How, for God's sake?"

Not for a moment did she fall for the story about the astronaut. Nor for the one about the embassy. The telephone conversation she took to be with another accomplice. And since her father owned a winery, she assumed I was inquiring about her Clermont address as part of a plan to kidnap her in exchange for a ransom. The psychologist made me swear not to breathe a word of this to Annabella.

"Maybe she'll feel like telling me herself," I said.

"Never, or perhaps ten years from now. You may know something about boys, but girls are different."

Another smile, and she was gone. I went to take care of our flight reservations. Only one seat left; I insisted there had to be two. Negotiations by telephone. Finally some VIP was persuaded to give up his seat. To Annabella. Fenner was in a hurry but offered to cancel some important meeting if I agreed to join him for lunch. I declined a second time. After Randy and the others had driven off, I inquired whether the girl and I could get a bite to eat in one of the airport facilities. The bars and cafeterias had all been closed down, but an exception was made in our case: we were now above the law. A man—dark-featured, bushy-haired, an undercover agent—escorted us to a small restaurant located on the other side of the departure area. Annabella's eyes were red and swollen: she'd been crying. Before long she started getting prissy. While the waiter was taking our order and I was debating what she should have to drink, she commented in a rather brisk, matter-of-fact tone that at home she was always served wine. She had on a blouse that was a couple of sizes too big, with rolled-up sleeves, and a pair of shoes that also looked a size too large. I was just beginning to enjoy the comfort of dry pants and the fact that I didn't have to stick to a diet of spaghetti any more, when I suddenly remembered her parents. There was a chance the news story might make the afternoon edition. We quickly drafted a telegram message, but when I got up from the table our cicerone sprang out of nowhere and offered to take care of it. When it came time to pay, we were treated as guests of the management. I tipped the waiter with the sort of generosity Annabella might have expected of a real astronaut. In her eyes I had suddenly become a celebrity and a hero—and a confidant, to the point where she even told me how she was dying to change clothes. Our chaperon escorted us to the Alitalia Hotel, where our luggage was already waiting for us in our room.

I had to hurry her along a little. At last, looking very prim and proper, she was ready, and with due decorum we embarked for the airplane. We were picked up by the airport's acting managing director—the managing director was temporarily indisposed, owing to a slight nervous breakdown—and driven out to the Cessna in one of the little Fiats used by the air controllers. At the foot of the ladder a rather courtly young Italian apologized for intruding and asked whether I cared for any souvenir photos of the recent drama. The photos would be forwarded to any address requested. I thought of the blond woman and thanked him anyway. A round of farewell handshakes. In the flurry of handshakes I could have sworn that I shook the same hand that had held me captive a short while ago.

I enjoyed flying in small planes. After a birdlike takeoff our Cessna veered northward. We landed at Orly shortly after seven. Annabella's father was there to meet her. Before landing we exchanged addresses, and to this day I still have fond memories of her. I wish I could say the same about her father. He was profusely grateful, even paying me a farewell compliment inspired no doubt by his having watched the television coverage of the "massacre on the steps." He said I had *esprit de l'escalier*.

Paris
(Orly–Garges–Orly)

I spent the night at Orly, at the Hotel Air France, since by now my contact had already left the Centre National de Recherche Scientifique and I didn't particularly feel like bothering him at home. Before going to sleep I had to get up and close the windows, because my nose was starting to act up again. It was then I realized I'd gone the whole day without sneezing once.

As it turned out I could have taken Fenner up on his offer, but then I'd been in such a hurry to reach Paris.

The next morning, the first thing after breakfast, I called the CNRS only to find out that my contact was on vacation, moving into a new house, but that he could still be reached. I then placed a call to his house in Garges, but it turned out he was just having his new phone connected. Announced or unannounced, I decided to pay him a visit. At the Gare du Nord the suburban trains were not in service, due to a strike. Seeing the mile-long line-up in front of the cabstand, I inquired about the nearest car rental agency—it turned out to be another Hertz—and settled for a Peugeot compact.

Trying to get around Paris, especially when you're unsure of your destination, is sheer hell. Not far from the Opéra—it wasn't on my itinerary; I wound up there quite by accident—a delivery van rammed into my bumper; the damage was so minor I kept on going, my mind now conjuring up visions of Canadian lakes and glacial waters as a distraction from the downpour of blazing-hot sun, unseasonable for this time of year. By mistake I wound up in a place called Sarcelles, one of those ugly, nondescript little settlements; then later I got stuck in front of a railway crossing, sweated, and pined after an air conditioner. Dr. Philippe Barth, my contact, was a well-known French computer scientist who also served as a scientific consultant for the Sûreté. The team he headed was in the process of programming a computer capable of solving multifactorial problems in which the number of case-related facts exceeded the storage capacity of the human memory.

The exterior of the house had just been freshly stuccoed. Surrounding the house was an old-fashioned garden: one wing shaded by stately elms, a gravel driveway, a flower bed in the center—marigolds, if I'm not mistaken (botany is the only subject astronauts are spared). Parked in front of a shed serving temporarily as a garage was a 2 CV, mud-spattered from the windows down, and right beside it a cream-colored Peugeot 604, its doors wide open, floormats spread out on the lawn, and dripping all over with soapsuds. Some kids were washing the car, but with such bustle and teamwork I had trouble counting them at first. They were all Barth's kids. The oldest two, a boy and a girl, greeted me in collective English: as soon as one began to falter, the ot'ier would fill in the missing word. How did they know they were supposed to speak English? A telegram had come from Randy announcing the arrival of an American astronaut. How could they tell I was the astronaut? No one else was in the habit of wearing suspenders. Good old Randy. While I was talking with the older kids, the younger one—I couldn't tell whether it was a boy or a girl—kept circling around me, hands folded behind its back, as if hunting for the spot that presented me in the most interesting light. I was told their father was very busy, and just as I was debating whether to go inside the house or to join the car-washing party,

Dr. Barth leaned out of the ground-floor window. He looked surprisingly young, but then I was still not accustomed to my own age. I was given a polite but restrained welcome, which made me wonder if I hadn't made a mistake in approaching him by way of the Sûreté, rather than the CNRS. But Randy was on friendlier terms with the police than with the scientific community.

Barth showed me into the library—his study was still in a state of chaos following the move—and then briefly excused himself while he went to change out of his varnish-stained smock. The house had been made to look like new already; rows of books stood freshly arrayed on the shelves, the smell of wax and varnish was everywhere. On the wall I noticed a blowup of Barth and his kids mounted on an elephant. Judging from the face in the photo I would never have guessed he was the promise of French computer science, but then I'd already had occasion to observe that people in the exact sciences tend to be less conspicuous in appearance than those in the humanities.

Barth came back into the room, frowning at his hands, which still showed traces of varnish, prompting me to suggest various ways of getting rid of the stains. We sat down by the window. I started out by saying I was neither a detective nor a criminologist, but that I had become involved in a rather bizarre and morbid case, and that I had come to him as a last resort. He was impressed by my fluent but not very European French. I explained that I was of French Canadian origin.

Randy had more confidence in my personal charm than I did. I was so anxious to gain this man's favor that I was somewhat embarrassed by the situation. The Sûreté was not a reference that he seemed to hold in particularly high esteem. Then, too, the attitude prevailing in academic circles is a decidedly anti-militaristic one. In such circles it's widely believed that astronauts are recruited from the armed forces, which was not always so, at least not in my case. But then I could hardly confide in him my whole life history. I was in doubt, therefore, as to what course I should take to break the ice. It wasn't till much later that he confessed to having been somewhat moved by the look of utter desperation on my face. My guess had been right: the colonel Randy had got to introduce me was in Barth's eyes a clown; nor was Barth exactly on the best of terms with the Sûreté. But sitting there in the library, I had no way of knowing that this indecision of mine was the best possible strategy.

He agreed to hear my story. I'd been involved with the case for so long I could have recited every detail from memory. I'd also brought along a set of microfilms containing all the documentation needed to illustrate my lecture, and Barth had just finished unpacking his projector. We plugged it in, leaving the windows and curtains open since the trees were already suffusing the room with a greenish half-light.

"It's a jigsaw puzzle," I began, feeding the first reel into the projector. "A puzzle consisting of numerous pieces; each of them is distinct enough on its own, but when fitted together they make for an indistinct whole. Not even Interpol has been able to crack the case. Just recently we conducted a simulation mission, the details of which I'll save till later on. The results were negative."

I was aware that his computer program was still in the experimental stage, that it had never been tested in the field, and that it was the subject of conflicting reports; but I was anxious to arouse his curiosity, and so I decided to give him a succinct version of the whole affair.

On June 27 of last year, the management of the Savoy Hotel in Naples notified the police that Robert T. Coburn, an American, aged fifty, had failed to return after setting out for the beach on the previous morning. His disappearance was all the more suspicious in that Coburn, a guest of the hotel for the past ten days, had been in the habit of going to the beach every morning, even walking the hundred-meter distance in his beach robe. That same evening his robe was found in his cabin by the beach attendant.

Coburn had the reputation of being an excellent swimmer.

Twenty years ago he had been a member of the American crawling team, and though he had a tendency to gain weight, he had managed to keep reasonably fit for a man his age. Since the beach was crowded, his disappearance went unnoticed. Five days later his body was washed ashore by the waves of a passing storm. His death would have been attributed to accidental drowning, a not unusual occurrence on every major beach, were it not for several minor details that later prompted an investigation. The dead man, a real-estate broker from Illinois, had no wife. Since he had died of unnatural causes an autopsy was performed, the results of which indicated that he had drowned on an empty stomach. Yet the hotel management claimed he had left for the beach right after breakfast. A minor discrepancy, perhaps, but the police commission was not on the best of terms with a group of city aldermen who had invested money in the renovation of certain hotels—among them the Savoy, which had recently been the scene of another incident, to be discussed later on. The police commission took a special interest in those hotels in which guests had met with accidents. A young assistant was put in charge of conducting a secret investigation, and he immediately placed the hotel and its guests under close surveillance. Being a freshly minted detective, he was anxious to sparkle in the eyes of his superior, and, thanks to his zealous enthusiasm, some very odd things were revealed. Coburn's daily routine had consisted of mornings at the beach, naps in the afternoon, then early-evening visits to the Vittorini brothers' health spa for the mineral-bath treatment that a local doctor, Dr. Giono, had prescribed for him—Coburn was being treated for the early stages of rheumatism. It also developed that during the week before his death Coburn had been involved in three car accidents, always on his way back from the Vittorini resort and each time under similar circumstances, namely, while trying to run a red light at an intersection. In every case the damage was minor, amounting to no more than dented fenders, and Coburn got off with only a fine and a warning. It was also around this time that he began eating supper in his room, rather than in the hotel dining room—before letting the waiter in, Coburn would first check through the door to make sure he was an employee of the hotel—and he soon gave up taking his daily stroll around the bay at sunset. These were indications that he felt harassed, even personally threatened—running a red light is a well-known method for shaking a tailing car—and such an interpretation would also explain why the deceased man had taken certain precautionary steps inside the hotel. But the investigation failed to turn up any further evidence. Coburn, whose childless marriage had ended in divorce fourteen years earlier, had made no friends either in the Savoy or downtown. It was later discovered that on the day before his death he had tried to buy a revolver from a local gun dealer, not realizing that by Italian law he was required to have a gun license. Since he didn't have one, he bought an imitation fountain pen designed to spray an attacker with a mixture of tear gas and an indelible dye. The pen was later found, still unwrapped, among his personal belongings, and so they were able to trace it back to the local retailer. Coburn had known no Italian, and the gun dealer had only a weak command of English. All that was learned was that Coburn had asked for a weapon capable of repelling a dangerous attacker, and not just some petty thief.

After establishing that all the accidents had occurred while Coburn was on his way back from the health spa, the assistant then proceeded to the Vittorinis. Because of the American's generosity toward the staff, they had no trouble remembering him. There had been nothing extraordinary about his behavior except that lately he had seemed more pressed for time, frequently ignoring the bath attendant's warning to wait ten minutes and dry off before going outside. Such meager findings failed to satisfy the investigating officer, who, in a fit of enthusiasm and inspiration, undertook a review of the establishment's books, which contained a record of payments made by all its bathing customers as well as those requiring hydrotherapeutic treatment.

Since the middle of May a total of ten Americans had visited the Vittorini spa, four of whom, like Coburn, had paid for a season pass (one could buy a one-, two-, three-, or four-week pass) but failed to show up after the eighth or ninth day. Not that there was anything particularly unusual about that, since any one of them might have been called away unexpectedly and thus had to forgo whatever refund he had coming. But now that the assistant knew their names, he decided to follow up his investigation. When later asked why he had limited himself to American citizens, he was not able to give a clear-cut answer. At one point he claimed he had hit on the idea of an American connection after learning that the police had recently smashed a narcotics ring trafficking in heroin between Naples and the States; on another occasion he said he had restricted himself to Americans for the simple reason that Coburn had been an American.

Of the four who failed to take full advantage of their subscriptions, the first, Arthur J. Holler, an attorney from New York, had suddenly left town after being notified of his brother's death. He was now back in his native city. Married and thirty-six years of age, he was employed as legal consultant for a large advertising agency.

The remaining three showed a certain physical resemblance to Coburn. In each case the person involved was a single male, between forty and fifty years of age, reasonably well-to-do, and invariably a patient of Dr. Giono. One of the Americans, Ross Brunner, Jr., had stayed at the same hotel as Coburn, the Savoy; the other two, Nelson C. Emmings and Adam Osborn, at boardinghouses that offered more modest accommodations but were also situated by the bay. Photos obtained from the States established beyond any doubt the physical resemblances of the missing: athletic builds, a tendency toward obesity, signs of balding, obvious attempts to camouflage same. Though Coburn's body was subjected to a thorough examination in the Institute of Forensic Medicine and showed no traces of violence, and though the cause of death was attributed to accidental drowning due to a muscle cramp or physical exhaustion, the police commission recommended in favor of continuing the investigation. Further inquiry was made into the fate of the other three Americans, and it was soon learned that Osborn had left Rome without notice, that Emmings had flown to Paris, and that Brunner had gone insane. Brunner's case was already a matter of police record. Though originally a guest of the Savoy, he had been lying in the city hospital since early May. He was an automobile designer from Detroit. During the first week of his stay in Naples he was a model of good behavior, spending mornings at the solarium and evenings at the Vittorini spa, except on Sundays, when he made a habit of going on various sightseeing tours. Since his trips were all arranged through a local travel agency, a branch of which was located in the Savoy, it was easy to establish his itineraries. Among the places he visited were Pompeii and Herculaneum; he took no sea baths, since his doctor had advised against it because of his kidney stones. Even though he had paid in advance, he canceled a trip to Anzio on the day before it was scheduled to leave; for the preceding two days his behavior had also been somewhat erratic. He gave up walking altogether, demanding his car even when his destination was only two blocks away, which turned out to be a nuisance because a new parking lot was then under construction and cars belonging to the guests had to be squeezed into a neighboring lot.

Brunner refused to pick up the car himself and insisted that it be brought around by one of the hotel staff; this gave rise to several altercations. That Sunday, he not only passed up the sightseeing tour but also failed to show up for supper, ordering through room service instead. No sooner did the waiter set foot inside the door than Brunner jumped him from behind and tried to strangle him. In the scuffle he broke one of the waiter's fingers before jumping out the window, suffering a broken leg and a fractured pelvis in the two-story fall. At the hospital he was diagnosed as having suffered—in addition to the multiple fractures—a mental blackout caused by an attack of schizophrenia. The hotel management was understandably anxious to hush up the whole affair. It was this incident in particular that prompted the commission's decision—following the death of Coburn—to widen the scope of the inquiry. The case now came under general review. The question arose whether Brunner had in fact jumped from the window, or whether he had been pushed. Yet no evidence could be found to challenge the waiter's credibility. He happened to be an elderly man with no criminal record.

Brunner remained in the hospital, not because of his mental condition, which gradually improved, but because of complications arising from the mending of his hip bone, while a relative who was supposed to come for him from the States kept postponing his visit. Finally, a prominent physician diagnosed Brunner's illness as insanity caused by an acute psychotic seizure of unknown etiology: the investigation had reached a dead end.

The second American, Adam Osborn, a middle-aged bachelor with a degree in economics, had driven an Avis rental car from Naples to Rome on June 5. In his hurry to leave the hotel, he had left behind such personal items as an electric razor, several brushes, a chest expander, and a pair of slippers. The management of the Savoy, wishing to forward his things, phoned the hotel in Rome where Osborn had made a reservation but was told that no one had checked in under that name. The hotel soon gave up trying to track down its capricious guest, but a more thorough investigation revealed that Osborn had never reached his destination. At the Avis rental agency the detective learned that the rental car, an Opel Record, had been found parked in the emergency lane in the vicinity of Zagarolo, just outside Rome—in perfect running condition and with Osborn's luggage still intact. Since the Opel belonged to and was registered with the firm's fleet in Rome—it had been delivered to Naples by a French tourist en route from Rome—the agency notified the Rome police. Osborn's things were seized, and the police in Rome decided to launch a separate investigation of their own when Osborn was found at dawn the following day—dead. He had been run over by a car on the Strada del Sole, at the Palestrina exit, roughly nine kilometers from where the rental car had been abandoned.

The assumption was that for no apparent reason he had climbed out of his car and started walking along the shoulder of the road until reaching the first exit, where he became the victim of a hit-and-run accident. The police were able to reconstruct the exact sequence of events, because Osborn had accidentally spilled some eau de cologne on the car's rubber matting; a police dog had little trouble in following the scent, even though it had rained during the night. It seems Osborn had kept to the side of the road the whole time except when the highway cut through a hill, at which point he had left the concrete road and climbed to the top of the nearest knoll. After a while he returned to the road and resumed hiking. When he came to the exit ramp, he went zigzagging down the road like a drunk. He died instantly of a fractured skull. The road was spotted with blood and strewn with splinters of headlight glass when they found the body. So far the police in Rome had been unable to track down the hit-and-run driver. The most curious thing of all was that, despite the heavy afternoon traffic, Osborn had been able to walk a distance of nine kilometers on the highway without being noticed. If nothing else, he should have attracted the attention of a highway patrol car, since pedestrians are not allowed on the highway. The explanation came a few days later, when a golf bag was found dumped early one morning in front of a police station and identified as Osborn's through the name engraved on the handgrips. This led to speculation that he might have been carrying the golf bag over his shoulder and that, because the clubs were covered by a hood and he himself was wearing a pair of jeans and a short-sleeved shirt, the passing drivers might have mistaken him for a member of the road crew. The clubs were probably left lying at the scene of the accident; whoever picked them up must have read about the investigation in the papers, panicked at the thought of becoming personally implicated in a criminal matter, and got rid of them.

Osborn's motive for abandoning the car and taking off with the golf clubs was still not known. The empty cologne bottle and traces of spilled cologne found on the floorboard suggested that he might have splashed the cologne on his face to ward off an attack of nausea or even a fainting spell. The autopsy failed to turn up any traces of alcohol or toxins in his blood. Before leaving the hotel Osborn had set fire to several sheets of hand-written stationery in a wastebasket. Though nothing could be salvaged from the ashes, they found among the items left behind an empty envelope addressed to the police, suggesting that at one point he had considered notifying the police but later changed his mind.

The third American, Emmings, was a press correspondent for United Press International. On a return trip from the Far East, where he had been on a recent assignment, he decided to stop over in Naples. He made a two-week reservation when he registered at the hotel but then unexpectedly left town on the tenth day of his stay. At the British European Airways agency he booked a seat on a Naples-London flight, and it took only one phone call to establish that immediately after landing in London he had committed suicide in one of the airport rest rooms. He shot himself in the mouth, and died three days later in the hospital without ever regaining consciousness.

The reason for his abrupt departure was completely legiti-mate: he had received a cable from UPI instructing him to con-duct a series of interviews in connection with rumors of a new scandal in Parliament. Emmings had the reputation of being a courageous and well-balanced man. He had served as a war correspondent in Vietnam, and before that as an apprentice reporter in Nagasaki following the Japanese surrender, where one of his eyewitness accounts had brought him instant fame.

Confronted with such facts, the assistant was eager to follow up his investigation by flying to London, the Far East, and even Japan, but instead he was instructed to interrogate those per-sons associated with Emmings during his stopover in Naples.

Emmings had traveled alone, so they again had to rely on the testimony of hotel personnel. His behavior revealed nothing out of the ordinary. But the maid recalled that while cleaning his room after his departure she had come across traces of blood in the washbasin and bathtub, as well as a bloody bandage on the floor. According to the autopsy report in London, Emmings had suffered a laceration on his left wrist. The cut was covered with a bandage and had a fresh scab. The conclu·ion reached was that Emmings had tried to commit suicide in the hotel by slashing his wrists but had then bandaged the wound before riding out to the airport. He, too, had taken the mineral baths, made daily trips to the beach, and toured the bay in a rented motorboat—in other words, had behaved in a most normal fashion.

Three days before he died, Emmings had gone to Rome to see a press attaché at the American embassy, an old acquaintance of his. The attaché later testified that Emmings had been in high spirits, but that on the way back to the airport he had never stopped glancing out the rear window, to the point where it became obvious. Jokingly he had asked Emmings if he'd made any enemies in Al Fatah. In reply Emmings had smiled and hinted he was on to something else, something he couldn't leak to anyone, not even to his friend, though it didn't really matter since it would soon be all over the front pages. Four days later he was dead.

Enlisting the help of several agents, the assistant went back to the health spa, this time to review the records of previous years. His presence at the Vittorini spa was becoming less and less welcome, since these constant invasions by the police were jeopardizing the establishment's good name. But when all the books were finally brought out into the open, eighteen new leads were uncovered.

Even though the pattern of events remained a mystery, the assistant began focusing his attention on men who were middle-aged foreigners and whose daily routine was suddenly interrupted some time between the second and third weeks of their stay.

Two of them turned out to be false leads. Both involved American citizens who had unexpectedly cut short their stay in Naples—one because a strike- had been declared at his company, the other because he had to appear in court as a plaintiff in a suit filed against a construction company accused of installing a defective drainage system on his property. The date of the hearing had been inexplicably moved up.

In the case of the owner whose company had been struck, the investigation was finally called off when it was learned that the owner had died and that a separate inquest was already under way as a matter of course. Eventually the police in the States reported the man had died of a cerebral hemorrhage exactly two months after his return trip to America. For years the deceased man had suffered from a cerebral vascular disease.

The next lead, the third, involved an actual criminal case that was never included in the official file because this American's "disappearance" was caused by his having been arrested by the local police. Acting on a tip from Interpol, the police uncovered a large amount of heroin on the suspect. He was presently awaiting trial in a Naples prison.

Three of the eight leads were thus eliminated. Two of the others seemed questionable. One involved a forty-year-old American who had come to the Vittorini spa for hydrotherapeutic treatment but who had stopped coming after injuring his spine in a water-skiing accident. The accident occurred while he was wearing a sailing kite harnessed to his back that allowed him to maneuver up and down on the towline; when the motorboat suddenly made an abrupt turn, the man came crashing down from a height of more than a dozen meters. Because of his injury he was laid up in a cast for a long time. The driver of the motorboat was also an American, a close friend of the victim; the incident still wasn't considered closed, because while convalescing in the hospital the man with the back injury developed a fever and began raving in delirium. The diagnosis wavered between some exotic disease contracted in the tropics and a delayed case of food poisoning.

The other questionable lead concerned a pensioner in his sixties, a naturalized American from Italy who had gone to Naples to collect his pension in dollars. He had been taking the mineral baths for his rheumatism when he suddenly interrupted the treatments, claiming they were bad for his heart. He was found drowned in the bathtub in his own apartment, exactly one week after his last visit to the spa. The autopsy ascribed the death to congestive heart failure and sudden cardiac arrest. Although the coroner uncovered nothing suspicious, the chief investigator, who had only stumbled on the case while checking the Vittorini records, ordered it reopened. Speculation arose that the pensioner might actually have been pushed under water: the bathroom door had been unlocked from the inside. An interrogation of the dead man's relatives failed to confirm any of these suspicions; not even a material motive could be established, since the pension was only a lifetime annuity.

Of the original eight leads only the last three led to the discovery of new victims, victims whose fates were typical of the evolving pattern. Again it was a matter of single men just past their prime, only now it was no longer restricted to Americans. The first was Ivar Olaf Leyge, an engineer from Malmö. The second was Karl Heinz Schimmelreiter, an Austrian from Graz. The third was James Brigg, a free-lance screenwriter identifying himself as an author, who, on his way over from Washington, had stopped off in Paris and contacted Olympia Press, a publisher that specialized in erotic and pornographic literature During his stay in Naples he boarded with an Italian family. His landlord and landlady knew nothing about him except what he himself had declared when he introduced himself, namely, that he was interested in exploring the "outer fringes of life"; it later came as news to them that he had been a regular visitor to the spa. On the fifth day he failed to return for the night. He was never again seen alive. Before notifying the police, the owners entered his room with a spare key to see what their tenant had left behind, only to discover that all his things were missing except an empty suitcase. They then recalled having seen their tenant leave the house every day with his briefcase full, only to return later with it empty. There was little reason to doubt their testimony, since the same family had been renting out rooms for years and enjoyed a spotless reputation. Brigg had been a bald man, of athletic build, with a face showing the scars of a harelip operation. He left no survivors, at least none who could be located. When he was later questioned, the publisher in Paris testified that Brigg had proposed writing a book exposing the seamier side of American beauty contests, a proposal the publisher had rejected as being too conventional. These statements could be neither confirmed nor denied. Brigg's disappearance had been so complete that no one could be found who had seen him since the day he vacated his room. Random inquiries made among the city's prostitutes, pimps, and junkies led nowhere. That was why the Brigg case was still classified as questionable; and, strange as it might sound, the only reason it was being kept on active file was that the man suffered from hay fever.

Not so the Swede and the Austrian, whose fates were never open to doubt. Leyge, a long-time member of the Himalaya Club and conqueror of Nepal's seven-thousand-foot range, had landed in Naples after divorcing his wife. He stayed at the Hotel Roma downtown, never went swimming, stayed away from the beach, made use of the solarium, took mineral baths, and made the rounds of the museums. Late in the evening of May 19 he left for Rome, even though he had originally intended to spend the entire summer in Naples. In Rome he left all his things in the car and headed straight for the Colosseum, where he climbed his way up to the highest tier and plunged down the outer wall. The coroner's verdict was "death due to suicide or accident as a result of a sudden mental blackout." A tall and well-proportioned blond, the Swede looked young for his age and was extremely fussy about his outward appearance and about keeping fit: tennis every morning at six, no drinking, no smoking—in short, a fanatic when it came to physical fitness. The divorce had been settled by mutual consent, with incompatibility as the reason. These facts were established with the help of the Swedish police to rule out sudden depression as a possible suicide motive following the breakup of a long marriage. It was later revealed that the couple had actually been separated for a number of years and had filed for divorce to make everything legal.

The story of the Austrian Schimmelreiter turned out to be more complicated. Although present in Naples since the middle of winter, he had not started the mineral bath treatment until April. Noticing a definite improvement in his condition, he had his ticket extended for the month of May. A week later he couldn't sleep, turned grumpy and irritable, and went around claiming that people were rummaging through his things; when his spare pair of gold-rimmed glasses disappeared and later turned up behind the sofa, he insisted it was the work of a thief. He had been living in a small boardinghouse and had been on friendly terms with his Italian landlady up to the time of his personality change, and so it was possible to get an exact description of his habits. On May 10 Schimmelreiter tripped on the stairs and had to spend some time in bed recuperating from a bruised knee. Within the space of two days he became more sociable, made up with his landlady, and, when his rheumatism refused to go away even after the pain in his knee subsided, resumed his trips to the baths. A few days later he had the whole boardinghouse on its feet with screams for help. Possibly imagining that someone was hiding behind the mirror—unlikely, since it was a wall mirror—he shattered it with his fist and tried to escape out the window. The landlady, unable to cope with the hysterical Schimmelreiter, called in a doctor acquaintance who made a diagnosis of coronary artery disease, a condition often leading to a minor stroke. The landlady insisted that the Austrian be transferred to the hospital. But while still at the boardinghouse he managed to smash the bathroom mirror and another one on the landing before being relieved of his walking stick. At the hospital he was given to fits of anxiety and crying spells and would try to hide under the bed, while frequent attacks of asthma—he was also an asthmatic—only made his condition worse. To one of the interns in charge of him he secretly confided that on two occasions an attendant at the Vittorini spa had tried to kill him by slipping poison into the bathing water and that this was surely the work of an Israeli secret agent. The intern debated whether he should include this information in the patient's medical chart. The ward doctor interpreted it as a symptom of a persecution complex arising from presenile dementia. Toward the end of May Schimmelreiter died of lung cancer. Not having any next of kin, he was buried in Naples at public expense, since his stay in the hospital had exhausted his funds. His case therefore represented an exception to the rule; in contrast to all the other victims, this one involved a foreigner who was financially destitute. Subsequent investigation revealed that during the war Schimmelreiter had served as a clerk in the concentration camp at Mauthausen and that he had stood trial following Germany's defeat but had escaped sentencing when the majority of witnesses, all of them former inmates of the camp, testified in his behalf. Although there were those who accused him of having beaten prisoners, their testimony was treated as third-hand evidence, and he was finally acquitted. And despite the apparent coincidence that his health had twice taken a turn for the worse following visits to the Vittorini establishment, the dead man's suspicions proved unwarranted, since there is no known poison capable of affecting the brain once it has been dissolved in bathing water.

The bathing attendant accused of having tried to poison the Austrian turned out to be a Sicilian, and not a Jew, and was in no way connected with Israeli intelligence.

Not counting the missing Brigg, the file now included the cases of six persons who had all met sudden deaths from random causes. Invariably the trail led back to the Vittorini health spa; and since there were a number of such spas in Naples it was decided to check their records as well. The investigation began to avalanche: the number of cases that had to be checked soon jumped to twenty-six, since it was quite common for people to discontinue the baths without demanding a refund, especially as the amount of money involved was usually quite small. The investigation proceeded slowly, because each and every lead had to be fully explored. Only when the subject turned up in good health was the case dropped.

Herbert Heyne, a forty-nine-year-old naturalized American of German origin and owner of a drugstore chain in Baltimore, landed in Naples around the middle of May. An asthmatic, he had been undergoing treatment for years in a number of sanatoria when a lung specialist prescribed sulfur baths as a precaution against rheumatic complications. He began his treatment in a small place located not far from his hotel on the Piazza Municipale, taking all his meals in the hotel restaurant where, nine days later, he created a scene by insisting the food tasted vilely bitter. After the episode in the restaurant he checked out of the hotel and traveled to Salerno, where he registered at a seaside resort. Late that same evening he decided to go for a swim. When the porter tried to talk him out of it because of the strong tide and poor visibility, Heyne insisted he would die not from drowning but from a vampire's kiss. He even showed him where the kiss of death would come—on the wrist. The porter, a Tirolese who began treating the guest as a fellow countryman the moment the conversation switched to German, went down to the beach when he heard Heyne crying for help. A lifeguard was found and the German was rescued, but when he began showing signs of madness—such as biting the lifeguard—they decided to have him transferred by ambulance to the hospital; there, in the middle of the night, he got up out of bed, smashed the windowpane, and started slashing his wrists with a sliver of broken glass. The nurse on duty alerted the staff just in time to save him from bleeding to death, but he came down with a severe attack of bronchial pneumonia and died three days later, without regaining consciousness. The inquest ascribed his suicide attempt to the state of shock caused by his near-drowning, which was also cited as the cause of his pneumonia. Two months later Interpol was brought into the case, when Heyne's Baltimore lawyer received a letter mailed by Heyne shortly before his departure from Naples stating that in the event of his sudden death the police should be notified at once because he suspected someone was plotting to kill him. The letter gave no other details except that the suspected killer was staying at the same hotel. The letter was sprinkled with a number of glaring Germanisms, although Heyne, a resident of the United States for twenty years, had a perfect command of English. This fact, along with certain discrepancies in the handwriting, made the lawyer dubious of the letter's authenticity—it had been written on hotel stationery—and after learning of his client's death, he went ahead and notified the authorities. The handwriting expert's report confirmed that Heyne had written the letter himself but in great haste and a state of extreme agitation. At this point the case was dropped.

The next case to come under review was that of Ian E. Swift, English-born, U.S. citizen, fifty-two, manager of a large furniture company in Boston, who landed by ship in Naples in early May, paid for a series of baths at the Adriatica, and stopped showing up after a week of visits; he stayed for a while at a cheaper hotel called the Livorno, then moved into the more luxurious Excelsior the same day he quit the baths. Witnesses were questioned in each of the hotels, but the testimony seemed to revolve around two different persons. The Swift at the Livorno spent most of the time in his room slaving over business correspondence, was an all-day boarder because it was cheaper, and occasionally went to the movies at night. The Swift at the Excelsior toured the local nightclubs in a hired, chauffeured car, traveled around in the company of a private detective, insisted on having his bed changed every day, had flowers sent to his hotel room, accosted girls on the street with invitations to join him for a ride and for supper, and went on periodic shopping sprees. He kept up this boisterous routine for four days. On the fifth day he left a note for the detective at the reception desk. When the detective finished reading the note in astonishment, he tried to reach Swift on the phone, but Swift refused to answer, even though he was in his room. He kept to his room the whole day, skipped lunch, and ordered dinner through room service. When the waiter appeared at the door, he found the room empty and heard Swift talking to him through a crack in the bathroom door. The same scene was repeated the following day—as if he couldn't stand the sight of the waiter. He kept up these antics until one day another man checked into the hotel, a man named Harold Kahn, an old friend and former business partner of Swift's who happened to be en route to the States after a long stay in Japan. Learning by chance that Swift was registered in the same hotel, he decided to pay him a visit, and forty-eight hours later they were both aboard a Pan Am jet bound for New York.

Though it lacked a fatal epilogue and therefore seemed to be an exception, Swift's case was nonetheless included in the series, since Swift really had Kahn to thank for his lucky trip home. The private detective testified that Swift had struck him as being not all there, that he was constantly talking about his negotiations with a terrorist organization called "The Terror of the Night," which he said he was prepared to finance if he was promised protection against a killer hired by one of his competitors in Boston. The detective was supposed to be a witness to these negotiations and act as a bodyguard. The whole thing sounded so preposterous that the detective's first impression was that his client must be on drugs. Swift's laconic note, in which a hundred-dollar bill had been enclosed, was in effect a letter of dismissal. He made no mention of his enemies except to say that they had come to pay him a visit at the Livorno, though in fact he had not received a single visitor there.

It was extremely hard to get any information out of Kahn concerning his meeting with Swift in Naples. Nor did the Americans have any reason to launch an investigation, since neither Swift nor Kahn had committed any crime. Both had returned to the States without incident, and Swift had gone back to his manager's job. Still the Italians persisted, in the hope that Kahn was in possession of certain facts that could possibly shed light on recent events. At first Kahn refused to talk; not until he was briefed on the case and given assurances of absolute confidentiality did he agree to make a deposition. His testimony proved disappointing to the Italians. It seems that Swift had welcomed Kahn in the most cordial manner but only after checking through the door to make sure it was he. He admitted with some embarrassment to having played a few "gags" and blamed it on the fact that he'd been drugged. Though outwardly calm and rational in his behavior, he refused to leave his room, because he said he'd lost all confidence in his detective and suspected him of having "gone over to the enemy." He had shown Kahn part of a letter in which someone had threatened to poison him unless a demand for twenty thousand dollars was met. When the letter was first sent to Swift at the Livorno, he had ignored the death threat, though rashly so, because the day after the deadline he felt so weak he could hardly get out of bed. For the better part of the day he was bothered by hallucinations and dizzy spells, so he wasted no time in packing and moving into the Excelsior. Realizing there was no easy way out of the extortion plot, he hired a private investigator, though without immediately divulging the purpose, because he first wanted to look him over and test him while living it up in the manner already described. The whole thing was somehow beginning to make sense, though it still didn't explain why Swift simply hadn't left town, especially when there was nothing keeping him in Naples. As Swift explained it, the mineral baths had proved so beneficial for his rheumatism that he was eager to complete the treatment.

At first Kahn was inclined to believe him, but after thinking over everything Swift had told him he began finding his friend's story less and less credible. The stories he had heard earlier from the hotel staff only confirmed his doubts. Had Swift been testing the detective that time he fired a gun at some flies during an orgy with several ladies of the night?—Kahn asked him straight out. Swift admitted it was true but repeated that the poison had left him temporarily deranged. Almost certain now that his friend had been stricken with some mental illness, Kahn decided to get him back to the States as fast as he possibly could. He settled Swift's hotel bill, bought plane tickets, and didn't leave Swift's side until they were both packed and on their way to the airport. Certain inconsistencies in the record suggest that Swift did not accept his friend's Samaritan kindness passively. The hotel staff testified that shortly before their departure the two Americans had had a serious quarrel. Whether or not Kahn had used physical force as well as verbal arguments, he would not volunteer any further information helpful to the inquiry, and the only solid piece of evidence, the letter, had disappeared. Kahn had seen only the first page, which had been typewritten—the illegible type made it look like one of a number of carbon copies—and full of grammatical mistakes in English. Back in the States, when he asked Swift what had happened to the letter, Swift broke out laughing and started opening a desk drawer as if he meant to show it to him, only to find it gone. The experts treated this latest evidence as a combination of the plausible and the implausible. Typing an extortion letter through several sheets of thick paper is a common practice, since once the individual letter traits have been obliterated in this way, it is next to impossible to trace the machine used. The fact that this was still a relatively recent practice unknown to most laymen seemed to argue in favor of the letter's authenticity. On the other hand, Swift's behavior all seemed inappropriate. A man who is being extorted doesn't react the way Swift did, not if he believes that the threats made on his life are actually going to be carried out. The experts finally concluded they were dealing with two overlapping factors: real coercion in the form of a shakedown attempt, apparently the work of a local resident (judging at least by the letter's poor English), and Swift's temporary insanity. If that was so, then the Swift case, when viewed within the context of the investigation's previous findings, only confused matters, since his apparent insanity otherwise conformed to the typical pattern.

The next one involved a Swiss by the name of Mittelhorn who arrived in Naples on May 27. His case differed from the others in that he was a familiar sight at the hotel, where he was an annual guest. The owner of a large secondhand bookshop in Lausanne and a well-to-do bachelor, he was a man given to certain eccentricities of behavior that were tolerated because he was considered such a desirable guest. He always occupied two adjoining rooms—one serving as an office, the other as a bedroom. Because of a food allergy, he always ordered specially prepared dishes and would carefully inspect the tableware before every meal. Whenever his face showed signs of swelling, a symptom commonly associated with Quincke's edema, he would summon the cook into the dining room and reprimand him severely. Yet the waiters claimed he was in the habit of eating between meals in some of the cheaper places downtown, where, although it was strictly against his diet, he would indulge his craving for fish soup, and then later take it out on the people at the hotel. During his most recent stay he had revised his habits somewhat. On his doctor's advice he had begun taking mud baths at the Vittorini spa, after suffering all winter long from rheumatism. In Naples he had his own private barber come regularly to the hotel, using no tools but those supplied by Mittelhorn himself, who refused to be touched by any blade or comb that had already been used on someone else. When hearing on his arrival this time that his barber had gone out of business, he became furious and never stopped complaining until he finally found another one he could trust.

On June 7 he requested that the fireplace in his room be lit. The fireplace served as a decorative piece and had never been used before, yet no one dared to question his order. His request was granted, although the temperature outdoors was quite high. The fireplace smoked a bit, but this did not seem to disturb him. That afternoon he locked himself in his room and skipped lunch, which was unprecedented, since he never missed a meal otherwise and was always so concerned about being punctual that he carried two watches, one on his wrist and another in his pocket. When he failed to answer either the telephone or the door, they had to force their way into his room—the lock had been jammed from the inside with a broken nail-file. They found him unconscious in the smoke-filled room. An empty bottle of sleeping pills suggested he had taken an overdose, so he was rushed to the hospital by ambulance. As he had been scheduled to go to Rome at the end of June to attend an auction, Mittelhorn had brought along a trunk containing rare and old prints. This was now empty, and the fireplace was full of charred sheets of paper. Folios of parchment not damaged by the fire had been cut into little strips with a pair of barber's scissors, and frames for mounting woodcuts had been completely demolished. None of the hotel property had been damaged except for a curtain cord that had been ripped out and made into a noose, indicating he had tried to hang himself but failed when the cord wasn't strong enough to support his weight. A stool placed next to the window provided still further evidence.

When Mittelhorn finally regained consciousness, after spending two days in a coma, his doctor, suspecting the early stages of congestive heart failure, asked for X-rays. That night Mittelhorn became restless and delirious. At one point he started screaming that he was innocent, that he was someone else; then he began making threatening gestures, as though he were fighting with someone, until he finally tried to jump out of bed. Unable to control him, the nurse ran to get the doctor. Mittelhorn, taking advantage of her momentary absence, slipped into the orderly room next to his isolation ward, smashed his fist through a windowpane in the medicine chest, and drank a whole bottle of iodine. He died three days later from severe internal burns.

The coroner's ruling was suicide caused by a sudden fit of depression. But when the investigation was later reopened and the hotel staff was subjected to a more thorough interrogation, the night porter referred to a curious incident that had taken place the evening before the crucial day. A box of stationery and envelopes was kept on the reception-desk counter for the convenience of guests and visitors. After dinner a messenger came to deliver an opera ticket to Mittelhorn's next-door neighbor, a German, who was out. The porter slipped the ticket into an envelope and stuck it into Mittelhorn's box by mistake. Stopping off for his key on the way up to his room, Mittelhorn was given the envelope, opened it, and took it over to a lamp in the lobby to read it. He collapsed into an armchair and covered his eyes. After a while, he glanced down again at the slip of paper in his hand, then hurried back to his room almost at a run. At that point the porter remembered the messenger with the ticket and, recalling having ordered the ticket himself over the phone, he realized it had been meant for the German and not for Mittelhorn. The sight of the German's empty box confirmed his mistake, and he decided to go directly to Mittelhorn's room. He knocked on the door but, getting no answer, went inside. The room was deserted. Lying on the table were the torn envelope and a crumpled piece of paper. The porter peeked into the envelope and found the ticket, which Mittelhorn had evidently overlooked. He took the ticket and, out of curiosity, smoothed out the sheet of stationery that had made such an impression on the Swiss. It was completely blank. The porter left the room, thoroughly bewildered, but said nothing when he later ran into Mittelhorn, who was on his way back from the refrigerator with a bottle of mineral water.

Since by now the investigation had reached the point of desperation, the detail of the blank sheet of paper began to acquire a special significance, all the more so as Mittelhorn had spent all of the following day burning his precious prints in the fireplace, coming downstairs only for lunch. Either the blank piece of paper had been a secret message or signal, or else he had experienced a hallucination in the hotel lobby and only imagined having read a nonexistent letter. The first possibility seemed highly implausible, smacking of some cheap movie thriller, and was not at all consistent with Mittelhorn's reputation as a man of unimpeachable honesty, a respected antiquarian, and an authority in his field. An audit of his business transactions turned up nothing the least bit shady or suspicious. As they probed deeper into the past, however, the investigation uncovered certain facts dating from the last world war. During it, Mittelhorn had been manager of one of Germany's largest secondhand bookshops, located in Munich. The owner of the shop was a rich and elderly Jew. When the Nuremberg laws went into effect, Mittelhorn was appointed sole trustee of the shop, and its former owner was shipped off to Dachau, where he eventually perished. After the war, Mittelhorn took legal possession of the shop, supporting his claim with a document designating him as sole heir and executor of the dead man's estate. But there were rumors that the document had been signed under duress and that Mittelhorn had had a hand in it. Two years later, even though these were only rumors, Mittelhorn transferred his business to Switzerland and settled permanently in Lausanne. Speculation arose that his mental breakdown was somehow connected with these events that had transpired some forty years ago, that, owing perhaps to an optical illusion, he mistook the blank sheet of paper for some communication reminding him of past sins, became so disturbed that he decided to destroy his most valuable possessions, and was eventually driven to the point of attempting suicide. On regaining consciousness in the hospital, he may have had a vision of the deceased; helpless against the dead man's reproaches, he was driven again to suicide. However plausible it may have been, such a hypothesis appeared too ingenious; above all it did nothing to explain how such a well-balanced man could suffer a sudden mental breakdown. When they interviewed Mittelhorn's former neighbor at the hotel, he merely confirmed the porter's testimony, namely, that he had failed to get the opera ticket and that by the time he did receive it the following day it was too late. The case of the eccentric antiquarian thus reached an impasse, like all the others.

The files now included nine cases, all following the same mysterious pattern and all ending in tragedy. Despite their all-too-obvious similarity, there were still insufficient grounds for launching a criminal investigation aimed at prosecuting the guilty, since there was not the slightest hint as to their where-abouts or whether in fact they even existed. One very curious incident took place soon after the Mittelhorn case was officially closed; the hotel turned over to the police a letter recently ad-dressed to the deceased man, even though he had been dead for more than a year. Postmarked Lausanne and bearing a type-written address, the letter contained a blank sheet of paper. Efforts to trace the letter failed. Nor could it have been some-one's idea of a practical joke, since the press had never made any mention of the first letter. I had my own thoughts on the matter, though I preferred not to reveal them for the time being.

Of the two remaining cases, the first dated from some time ago, the second was more recent. To start with the older one, some years ago, in May, a German from Hanover, Johann Titz, took a room in Portici, not far from Herculaneum. He chose a small boardinghouse with a spectacular view of Vesu-vius, because as a postcard manufacturer he was interested in producing a series of cards devoted to Vesuvius. But he was also there for medical reasons: he had suffered from asthma since his childhood. After too much exposure to the sun, he came down with a severe case of heat blisters. A dermatologist whom he consulted in Naples advised against any more sun-bathing. To the doctor's astonishment, his patient vehemently objected, insisting that the sunbathing was absolutely indispen-sable for clearing up his asthma and that it had been recom-mended by his doctor in Hanover. Titz was taking mud baths in a small spa to which he commuted every day from Hercu-laneum—he had driven down from Germany in his own car.

On May 9 he began having dizzy spells and attributed them to food poisoning. He accused his landlady of serving him contaminated fish and threatened not to pay his bill. But in the end he paid it and drove off. When the landlady later went to clean his room, she found a message inscribed on the wall in red India ink: "I was poisoned here." The ink had penetrated so deeply into the plaster that there was no getting rid of it except by repainting the walls, so the owner of the boardinghouse filed a complaint against her former tenant.

On his way north, however, somewhere in the vicinity of Milan, Titz suddenly swerved to the left on a straight stretch of highway, cut across a grass island, and, disregarding the blinking lights and honking horns of the other drivers, started driving down the opposite lane into the path of the oncoming traffic. Astonishingly enough, he was able to drive like this for a distance of four kilometers, forcing the oncoming cars into the most desperate tactical maneuvers. Some of these drivers later testified that he seemed to be aiming for the "right" car. To avoid a long-haul Intratrans truck blocking his path, he swerved onto the island, waited till the truck had passed, then moved back into the wrong lane, where, less than a kilometer down the road, he collided with a small Simca carrying a young couple and a child. The child, though critically injured, was the sole survivor. Titz, who had been driving at high speed without a safety belt, died behind the wheel. There was speculation in the press that this was a new form of suicide in which the suicide victim tried to take others with him. In a collision involving the huge tractor-trailer he would probably have been the sole fatality, which explained why he had passed up the "chance." The case was classified as definitely belonging to the series when reports came in concerning certain incidents that had taken place immediately prior to the accident. Just outside Rome, Titz had pulled in at a service station because of apparent engine trouble and pleaded with the mechanics to hurry because he said the "red bandit" was on his tail. At first the mechanics thought he was joking, but they changed their minds when he promised each of them ten thousand lire if they could fix his engine in fifteen minutes, and then actually kept his promise. When he gave all of the nine mechanics on duty the same "bonus," they decided he was not all there. He might have gone unidentified had it not been that while he was backing out of the garage the German put a dent in one of the cars parked outside and drove off without stopping, though not before they were able to take down his license-plate number.

The last case dealt with Arthur T. Adams II, who checked into the Hotel Vesuvio in Naples, bought a three-week pass to the mineral baths, then dropped out a few days later when he discovered he was allergic to sulfur. At forty-nine, he was a tall and easygoing man, always on the move and something of a restless type, having tried his hand at some ten different jobs. At one time or another he had been a bank officer, a Medicare official, a piano salesman; he had taught correspondence courses in banking, worked as a judo and later as a karate instructor, and actively pursued a number of hobbies: he was a licensed parachutist and an amateur astronomer, and for the past year or so he had been publishing on an irregular basis *The Arthur T. Adams II Newsletter,* featuring editorials on a wide range of subjects of personal concern to its publisher. Copies of the newsletter were run off on a duplicating machine at his own expense and distributed free of charge to several dozen acquaintances. He was also a member of a number of different societies, ranging from a dianetics circle to an organization for hay-fever sufferers.

Adams first began acting suspiciously on his return trip to Rome by barreling along at high speed, then pulling over in deserted places; buying an inner tube when his car used tubeless tires; sitting out a storm in a parked car just outside Rome; and telling a highway patrolman his windshield wipers were broken when there was actually nothing wrong with them. That night he arrived in Rome and made the rounds of the hotels, looking for a vacancy—even though he had already reserved a room at the Hilton—returning to the Hilton only when he failed to find any. The next morning he was found lying dead in his bed. The autopsy disclosed early emphysema, enlargement of the heart, and generalized hyperemia typical of death due to suffocation. The actual cause of death was never determined. The coroner's report suggested either overstimulation of the parasympathetic nervous system or suffocation caused by cardiac arrest precipitated by a severe asthmatic attack. For a while the case came under discussion in various medical journals, where the coroner's ruling was attacked as erroneous. It was argued that only infants have been known to die of pillow suffocation, whereas an adult will immediately awaken if his nose and mouth are obstructed. Nor was there any evidence to substantiate the claim that he had suffered an asthmatic attack. Finally, there was the position of the body: Adams was found lying on his stomach, with both arms wrapped around his pillow and the pillow pressed flat against his face. But if it was a suicide, then it had no precedent in the records of forensic medicine. Some tried to attribute his death to extreme fright, but, although such cases have been known to occur, no one has yet proved nightmares to be a cause of death. After a long delay, Interpol finally decided to intervene when two letters turned up in the States, both mailed by the deceased to his former wife, with whom he remained on friendly terms following their divorce. The letters had been mailed three days apart, but they arrived at the same time because of the backlog of mail created by a postal strike. In the first letter Adams wrote he was depressed and that he was having hallucinations of the "sugar cube" variety. This was a reference to the period preceding their divorce, when Adams and his wife had been in the habit of taking psilocibin dished up in sugar cubes. Now, five years later, he had no idea what was causing these "freaky" hallucinations, which occurred mainly at night. The second letter was altogether different in both tone and content. He was still having hallucinations, but he was no longer alarmed now that he knew what was causing them.

> A detail you'd never suspect as being important has led me to the most incredible discovery. I've managed to get my hands on some material for a series of articles dealing with a completely new type of crime, a crime that's not only unmotivated but also indiscriminate, in the same way that scattering nails all over the road is an indiscriminate crime. You know I'm the last person to exaggerate, but the press won't be the only ones to sit up and take notice when I start publishing this stuff. But I've got to be careful. This material is too hot to keep around here. Don't worry, though; I've got it stored someplace where it's good and safe. Not another word till I get back. Will write from Rome as soon as I can. This is the sort of bonanza every journalist dreams about. And what a lethal one it is.

There's no need for me to elaborate on the intensive search that was made into the whereabouts of Adams's secret hiding place. The search proved to be a waste of time. Either he didn't know anything and the letter was just another one of his hallucinations, or he had done too good a job of hiding the material.

Adams's death brings to a close the list of tragic events originating in and around Naples. Besides the Italians, the investigation involved the law-enforcement agencies of Sweden, Germany, Austria, Switzerland, and the United States, who were drawn into the case because of the victims' nationality. Interpol, which was supervising and coordinating the case, revealed a number of irregularities and minor omissions in the course of their investigation—such as failing to report missing hotel guests right away, or neglecting to perform an autopsy despite indications of a violent death—but in no instance were they able to establish any criminal motives, attributing the mistakes either to sloppiness, to negligence, or to self-interest.

Interpol was the first to resign from the case, with all the other agencies—including the Italian—following suit. It was reopened only on the initiative of Mrs. Ursula Barbour, Adams's chief executor. Adams had left an estate worth ninety thousand dollars in stocks and bonds, and Mrs. Barbour, a woman in her eighties who had been Adams's foster mother, decided to use a part of the estate for apprehending the murderers of the man she regarded as her son. After familiarizing herself with the circumstances of his death, in particular with that last letter addressed to his former wife, she became thoroughly convinced that he was the victim of a crime so cunningly executed it had defied the efforts of all the various international agencies combined.

Mrs. Barbour turned the matter over to Elgin, Elgin, and Thorn, a respectable agency headed by Samuel Ohlin-Gaar, a lawyer and former friend of my father's. This was around the time when the end of my career as an astronaut was already inevitable. After Ohlin-Gaar's people had reviewed all the files, checked every possible lead, and gone to considerable expense to consult the most eminent authorities in criminology and forensic medicine, and still failed to make any progress, Ohlin-Gaar, acting on the advice of one of his oldest associates—a man by the name of Randolph Loers, better known to his friends as Randy—decided, more out of desperation than hope, to mount a simulation mission, that is, to send to Naples an unmarried American matching the type of victim in every possible way. At that time I was a frequent guest at old man Ohlin's place, and one day he began filling me in on the case in a casual sort of way, insisting it was not a violation of professional secrecy to do so since by now the only alternative to carrying out a simulation mission was to wash one's hands of the whole affair.

At first I didn't take the thought of my eligibility too seriously, but then it turned out the job was mine for the asking. It so happened that I was fifty and—except for an occasional touch of rheumatism and of course my hay fever—in top physical condition. Since it looked so tempting from across the ocean, I volunteered for the mission. Three weeks ago, using the alias of George L. Simpson, a broker from Boston, I landed by plane in Naples, where I checked in at the Vesuvio, bought a pass to the Vittorini spa, got a suntan, and played lots of volleyball. To make it look as authentic as possible, I used some of Adams's personal things, which Mrs. Barbour had been saving. During the time I was in Naples, a six-man team kept me under constant surveillance—two men to a shift, plus two technicians to monitor my blood, heart, and lungs. I wore electronic sensors wherever I went, except on the beach, where a pair of well-hidden binoculars was deployed. As soon as I arrived I put nineteen thousand dollars in the hotel safe: five days later I picked up the money, and kept it in my room from then on. I wasn't shy about making friends; I visited the same museums as Adams, went to the opera as he had, followed his footsteps around the bay, and drove to Rome in the exact same Hornet. To increase the range of the sensors, the car was equipped with an amplifier. A specialist in forensic medicine, Dr. Sidney Fox, was waiting for me in Rome. His job was to examine all the medical data recorded on the tapes, which he did, and that's how the mission ended—a complete flop.

What I had given Barth was an abbreviated version of the case, the one we always used when it became necessary to enlist the services of an outsider. We called it "the panoramic variant."

The windows of the study faced the north, and the shade thrown by the giant elms made the room even darker. I disconnected the projector, Barth switched on the desk lamp, and the room was immediately transformed. He said nothing, with only his eyebrows registering mild astonishment, and suddenly I realized the utter futility of my having intruded on a complete stranger. I was afraid he was going to ask how I thought he could be of help—assuming he didn't simply dismiss the whole thing out of hand. Instead he got up, paced up and down the room, then came to a stop behind a handsome antique chair, placed his hands on its carved back rest, and said:

"You know what you should have done? Sent a whole group of simulators down there. No fewer than five."

"You think so?" I asked with some bewilderment.

"Of course. If we conceive of your mission in terms of a scientific experiment, then you failed to fulfill either the preliminary or the accessory conditions. Either *you* were deficient or your environment was. In case you were the cause, then you should have selected men having the same characteristic variability ratio as that exhibited by the victims."

"Aptly put!" The words slipped out of my mouth.

He smiled.

"You're not accustomed to our language, I see. That's because you associate with people who have a policeman's mentality. That mentality is all right for prosecuting criminals but not for proving whether in fact a criminal exists. I suspect if your life had been in danger you wouldn't have noticed it. Up to a point, of course. Later you'd have been aware of the accompanying circumstances but not of the causality itself."

"Aren't they one and the same?"

"They can but need not be."

"But I was ready for that. I was supposed to record anything that looked the least bit suspicious."

"And what did you record?"

I smiled in embarrassment.

"Nothing. Oh, once or twice I was tempted to, but then I realized it was a case of too much introspection."

"Have you ever used hallucinogens?"

"In the States, before joining the mission. LSD, psilocibin, mescaline—all under medical supervision."

"I see . . . part of your training. And would you mind telling me what you hoped to achieve by taking on the part? You personally."

"Hoped to achieve? I was fairly optimistic. I thought we

could at least prove whether it was a crime or just a matter of coincidence."

"You *were* optimistic, weren't you. Naples is a trap, there's no doubt about that. But one that operates like a lottery, not like a machine. The symptoms tend to fluctuate, to behave erratically. They can subside or disappear altogether, right?"

"Absolutely correct."

"All right, suppose now we take a firing zone as a model. You can be killed either by someone deliberately aiming at you or by the sheer density of fire. But either way someone on the other end is anxious to see a lot of people dead."

"Oh, I see what you're driving at. The element of chance doesn't rule out the possibility of a crime, is that it?"

"Precisely. You mean to say that was never considered?"

"Not really. Someone once raised the possibility, but the reply was that if that were the case it would mean having to revise the whole method of investigation. . . ."

"Either a wicked man or a wicked fate, is that it? But even the expression *corriger la fortune* has become proverbial. Why didn't you hook up a two-way transmission?"

"Too much of a bother. I couldn't go around loaded down with a lot of electronic equipment. Besides, there was another catch, one that came up in connection with the Swift case— Swift was the one rescued by the friend who had registered at the same hotel. Swift made his hallucinations sound so convincing he almost had his friend believing them."

"I see what you mean. *Folie à deux*. In other words, you didn't want to risk having your shadow fall for any of your hallucinations, is that it?"

"Exactly."

"Correct me if I'm wrong. Of the eleven victims, two escaped alive, and then there's another who is still missing. The missing man's name is Brigg. Am I right?"

"Correct. Brigg would have been the twelfth. He hasn't been definitely classified yet."

"Due to insufficient evidence, I suppose. Now we come to

their chronological order. In this respect your summary is misleading. It presents the individual cases in the order of their discovery, which is something completely incidental, rather than in the order of their occurrence. What was the time span involved? Two years?"

"Yes. Titz, Coburn, and Osborn passed away two years ago. Brigg disappeared around the same time. The rest date from last year."

"Any this year?"

"If there have been any, we wouldn't know about them till the fall. Especially since the original investigation has been discontinued."

"Assuming your facts are correct, then it would seem to be an expanding series. Three in the first set, eight in the second. Well, well . . . I see you weren't acting as a decoy only in Italy."

"Meaning?"

"That you've been trying to bait me, too. And I have to admit it's tempting! Your version makes everything seem crystal clear. The pattern is all too obvious. But the fact that it has everybody stumped leads me to believe there's more to it than meets the eye. Although the more one hears of the case histories, the more one begins to suspect some form of unmotivated insanity. Wouldn't you agree?"

"Yes. On that point there's general agreement. Otherwise they wouldn't have called off the investigation."

"So why should there be any doubt that a crime has been committed?"

"How should I put it . . . it's like looking at a photo—I'm thinking now of a halftone. The naked eye can make out the general outline but not the details. A magnifying glass will make some things stand out more clearly, but the image will remain blurred. If we take it to the microscope we find the picture gets lost, that it disintegrates into tiny dots. Each dot is something distinct; they no longer combine to a meaningful picture."

"Are you suggesting that once you've accepted the hypothesis of a random series of poisonings, the more detailed the examination the flimsier the hypothesis?"

"Precisely."

"And the same thing applies if you assume the existence of a culprit?"

"The same thing applies. The conclusion is almost always the same: not one of the victims was poisoned by someone else, and not one of them had the means to do it himself. But the fact still remains . . ."

I shrugged my shoulders.

"So then why do you always insist on its being either a crime or a coincidence?"

"What alternative is there?"

"Maybe there is one." He picked up a copy of *France-Soir* from his desk. "Have you read today's papers?"

He showed me the headlines in bold print: BOMB EXPLODES IN THE LABYRINTH—MASSACRE ON THE STEPS—TEEN-AGED GIRL RESCUED BY UNIDENTIFIED MAN.

"Yes," I replied. "I'm familiar with what happened."

"There you have it. The classic example of a modern crime. Premeditated and at the same time accidental. Anyone standing in the vicinity automatically became a victim."

"But that's not quite the same thing!"

"Granted, it's not. The victims in Naples were predestined for death because of certain personality traits, but not those at the airport. Fair enough. But what about the case of that man Adams who wrote his wife about the possibility of a random crime, and who compared it to covering a road with nails. Obviously it was a crude analogy. But it's just as obvious that whoever's behind these deaths is anxious to create the impression he doesn't exist."

I withheld comment. Barth gave me a quick glance, stood up, paced around the room, then sat down again and asked:

"What's your own personal opinion?"

"I can only tell you what struck me most. Suppose the cause of death was poisoning; wouldn't you expect the symptoms to be the same in every case?"

"Well, weren't they? I was of the impression they all followed a pattern. First the phase of excitement and aggression, then the hallucinating phase, most often associated with a persecution mania, and finally the withdrawal phase—withdrawal either from Naples or from life itself. Either they tried to escape by car, plane, or on foot, or they resorted to a piece of glass, a razor blade, a cord, a bullet in the mouth, a bottle of iodine. . . ."

I had the suspicion he was trying to impress me with the power of his memory.

"I'll admit they were similar. But when you start looking into the backgrounds . . ."

"Go on."

"Well, as a rule, the manner of death has nothing to do with the personality of the deceased. Whether a person dies of pneumonia, cancer, or in a car accident is not something determined by his personality. Of course there are exceptions, as in the case of a test pilot's occupational death, but as a rule there's no correlation between the way a person dies and the way he lives."

"In short, death is unrelated to personality type. Go on."

"But here it is related."

"Ah, now you're feeding me demonology! Just what are you implying?"

"Exactly what I said. A champion swimmer dies in a drowning accident. A mountain climber falls to his death. A car fiend gets killed in a head-on collision."

"Hold on! Which one was the car fiend—Titz?"

"Yes. He owned three cars, two of them sports cars. To continue: a coward is killed while running away. . . ."

"Who was that?"

"Osborn. The one who abandoned his car and was taken for a member of the road gang."

"You didn't mention anything about his being a coward."

"I'm sorry. The version I gave you left out many details. Osborn was in the insurance business, was heavily insured himself, and was known as a man who avoided taking any risks. The first time he felt threatened he sat down and wrote a letter to the police, then lost his nerve and took off. Adams, the eccentric, died as he lived—in an unconventional manner. The heroic reporter stuck it out till the end and then shot himself. . . ."

"Wasn't he trying to escape, too?"

"I don't think so. He had orders to fly to London. He suffered a momentary breakdown, tried to slash his wrists, then patched himself up and flew off on his new assignment. When he saw he wasn't up to it, he shot himself. He must have been a very proud man. I have no idea how Swift would have died. As a young man he was known for being wishy-washy, a typical prodigal son, a dreamer, always in need of someone stronger than himself. A wife, a friend. It was the same way in Naples."

Barth sat there with wrinkled brow, tapping his chin, and stared absently into space.

"Well, that's easy enough to explain. A case of regression, of reversion to an earlier time period . . . I'm not a specialist in this area, but I believe that some hallucinogens . . . What was the consensus of the toxicologists? Of the psychiatrists?"

"Certain symptomatic analogies with LSD, except that LSD does not have such individualized effects. Pharmacology has no record of such a drug. The deeper I delved into their individual backgrounds, the more I saw that not one of them had acted contrary to his nature—quite the opposite, that each had revealed it in grotesquely exaggerated form. A man who's careful with money becomes a penny pincher. A pedant—I'm referring now to the rare-book dealer—spends the whole day cutting up a trunkful of papers into little strips. Examples abound. If I could leave you the files, you'd see for yourself."

"By all means. So this factor X would have to be something on the order of a 'personality drug.' Right . . . But such an approach won't bring us any closer to a solution. Psychological analysis can tell us how the factor behaves, but not how it infiltrates the victim."

He was leaning forward in his chair, his head lowered and his eyes fixed on his hands, which were cupped around his knees. Suddenly he looked me straight in the eye.

"I'd like to ask you a personal question. May I?"

I nodded.

"What was it like during the simulation? Were you confident the whole time?"

"No. It was altogether an awkward situation, not at all as I had imagined it would be. Not because I was using a dead man's things—I got used to that in a very short time. Because of my profession, I was considered tailor-made for the mission."

"Is that so?" His eyebrows shot up.

"The public imagines it to be fascinating, but except for a few brief moments of excitement it's all routine—boring and monotonous routine."

"I see. In much the same way as in Naples, right?"

"Yes, especially since we're also trained in the art of self-analysis. If instruments are always subject to error, then the final indicator has to be man."

"Monotonous routine, you say. In what ways were you excited in Naples? When and where?"

"When I was afraid."

"Afraid?"

"At least twice. And each time it gave me something of a thrill."

The words did not come easily, for I was dealing in intangibles. He never took his eyes off me.

"Did you enjoy being afraid?"

"I can't give you a yes or no answer. It's best when a person's abilities coincide with his ambitions. My ambitions have always tended toward the impossible. There's an infinite variety of risks, but I personally have never been attracted by such ordinary risks as, say, Russian roulette. That sort of test strikes me as jejune. On the other hand, I've always had a great attraction for the unknown, the unpredictable, the undefinable."

"Is that why you decided to become an astronaut?"

"I don't know. Maybe that's the reason. People think of us as clever chimpanzees guided by a remote-control computer. The highest order, the symbol of our civilization, whose opposite pole you see before you." I pointed to the paper featuring a front-page photo of the escalator. "I don't believe that's necessarily true. And even if it were true, we'd have been all alone on Mars, completely on our own. I knew all along my physical disability would hang over me like the sword of Damocles. For six weeks out of the year, during the blooming season, I'm totally worthless. Still, I was counting on the fact that since no vegetation grew on Mars, which everybody, including my superiors, took for granted . . . but anyhow it was the hay fever that got me demoted to the backup crew, where I knew I didn't stand a chance."

"Of flying to Mars?"

"That's right."

"And did you go on being a backup member?"

"No."

"*Aut Caesar aut nihil.*"

"That's one way of putting it."

He unclasped his hands and sank deeper into his armchair. Sitting there with eyelids half open, he seemed to be digesting my words. Then a twitch of the eyebrows and a flicker of a smile.

"Let's return to earth. Did all the victims have allergies?"

"Just about, though in one case it was never substantiated. The allergies varied, dust allergy being the most common, followed by asthma. . . ."

"And when was it you were afraid? A moment ago you mentioned . . ."

"I remember two different occasions. The first time was in the hotel restaurant, when another Adams was paged to the phone. I knew it was a popular name, I knew they were paging someone else; still, for a moment I had the feeling it wasn't just a coincidence."

"You had the feeling they were paging a dead man, is that it?"

"Not at all. I thought it was the start of something. That it was a code word being used so none of the other customers would be the wiser."

"Did it ever occur to you it might have been someone from your own team?"

"Out of the question. Under no circumstances were they to get in touch with me. Only in the event of a catastrophe, say, a declaration of war, was Randy, our leader, supposed to approach me directly. But only under such conditions."

"Excuse me for being so inquisitive, but this strikes me as important. So Adams was paged. But what if the caller really had you in mind; wouldn't that mean he saw through your disguise and was telling you as much?"

"That's exactly why I was so scared. I was even tempted to go to the phone."

"What for?"

"To make contact with the other side. Better that than nothing at all."

"I see. But you didn't go, did you?"

"No. The real Adams beat me to it."

"And the second time?"

"That was during my one night in Rome, at the hotel. I was staying in the room where Adams had died in his sleep. Oh yes, there's something else I should explain. You see, various simulation roles were considered. I didn't have to pose as Adams, there were alternate roles, but I sat in on the meetings and tipped the scale in favor of Adams—"

I broke off, seeing Barth's eyes momentarily light up.

"Let me guess. It wasn't the temporary insanity, it wasn't the seaside, and it wasn't the highway. It was just the thought of that safe and secluded hotel room—the solitude, the comfort, and death. Am I right?"

"Possibly, though I wasn't aware of it at the time. I guess they thought I was hoping to find the secret disclosures he was supposed to have stashed away somewhere, but that wasn't it at all. The truth was, I found the man somehow likable."

Even though he'd stung me a moment ago with his "*Aut Caesar aut nihil,*" I found myself being a lot more talkative than usual, so dependent was I on this man's help. Exactly when this whole affair had become an obsession with me I couldn't say. At first I'd treated the impersonation as just another routine exercise, as a necessary part of the game. I don't know at what point it had pulled me in so completely that at the same time it pushed me away. I was looking forward to the danger, counting on it; I knew it wasn't my imagination; but just when I seemed to be on the verge of it, it turned out to be an illusion. I was barred from it. I'd done everything Adams had done—everything except share the same fate, and that's why I had nothing to show for it. Maybe Barth's remark had offended me so much because it touched on the truth. One of Fitzpatrick's medical colleagues on the Mars project, Kerr, a Freudian, would have said I was trying to force a showdown, that I preferred death to defeat; in other words, he'd have explained my choice of Adams, the mission itself, in terms of a Freudian death wish. You can bet that's what he would have said. But who cares. Asking for this Frenchman's help was tantamount to violating the mountain climber's code: I was giving him the lead so he could pull me up on the rope. But better that than total disaster: I had no intention of winding up a loser.

"Let's talk about methodology." Barth's voice roused me from my thoughts. "First of all, the class of victims, the mode of differentiation. In this regard you proceeded far too arbitrarily."

"What makes you think so?"

"The fact that the incidents didn't form categories of their own but were arbitrarily categorized as relevant or irrelevant. Your criteria were death and insanity, or at least insanity, even when the latter failed to result in death. Compare the behavior of Swift and Adams. Swift, you might say, went publicly insane, whereas if it hadn't been for Adams's letter to his wife, you never would have found out about his hallucinations. And there's no telling how many other cases there were like that."

"Excuse me," I said, "but that's inevitable. What you've just accused us of is the classic dilemma of every investigation into the unknown. Before its limits can be defined the agent of causality must be identified, but before the agent of causality can be identified one must first of all define the subject under investigation."

He looked at me with undisguised approval.

"Well, well, I see you're well versed in the language, too. But it surely wasn't the detectives who taught it to you, now was it?"

I said nothing in reply. He sat rubbing his chin.

"Yes, that is indeed the classic dilemma of induction. But let's turn to some of the discarded facts, to the false clues. Were there any promising leads that in the end proved useless?"

Now it was my turn to look at him with approval.

"Yes, one very interesting one. We really had our hopes pinned on it. Before leaving for Italy all of the American victims had been patients at one of Dr. Stella's clinics. You've heard of Dr. Stella, I suppose?"

"No, I haven't."

"People say different things about him—some consider him to be one of the best, others claim he's a quack. Whenever one of his patients was suffering from rheumatism, he would prescribe the mineral baths in Naples."

"What!"

"I jumped, too, when I heard that, but it turned out to be a false lead. He considered the baths around Vesuvius to be far and away the best, even though we have more than our share in the States. The ones who were talked into making the trip were in the minority, for it isn't true that all Americans are spendthrifts. If a patient said he couldn't afford a trip to Vesuvius, Stella would send him to an American health spa. We tracked down these people—they numbered about a hundred— and found them all safe and sound. Some of the patients were just as handicapped as before, but in any case we didn't come across a single fatality of the Italian type. Most of them died of natural causes—heart disease, cancer. . . ."

"I assume they were married, had families of their own," said Barth, distracted by some thought or other.

I couldn't help smiling.

"Doctor, now you're resorting to the same kind of crazy parlance, the same clichés, as those people in the agency. . . . As a matter of fact, most of them did have families, but then there was no shortage of widowers and old bachelors among them, either. Besides, since when are wives and children an antidote? And an antidote against what?"

"You can't reach the truth without crossing a sea of mistakes," Barth said sententiously but with a wry look in his eye. "And do you happen to know how many patients this Dr. Stella sent to Naples?"

"Yes, I do know. And this is one of the most bizarre coincidences of all. Every time I think about it I feel like I'm on the verge of cracking the case. Altogether he sent twenty-nine rheumatic patients, including five of our Americans: Osborn, Brunner, Coburn, Heyne, and Swift."

"Five of the seven Americans?"

"That's right. Neither Emmings nor Adams had gone to Stella's clinic for treatment. Nor had Brigg, but then, as you know, he was never classified as a victim."

"This is all extremely relevant. And the other twenty-four patients?"

"I know the statistics by heart. Sixteen of them had been sent before any of the incidents in question had taken place. All returned safely to the States. Last year he sent thirteen. Five of the victims came from this group."

"Five of the thirteen? And of the eight who survived, were there any conforming to the 'model victim'?"

"Three of them, in fact. All single men, financially well off, and in their fifties. All safely returned. All alive."

"Only men? Didn't Stella ever treat women?"

"He did treat women. Prior to the deaths in question he sent four women to Italy, two just last year. None this year."

"How do you explain this disproportion between the sexes?"

"Stella's clinics first became famous as treatment centers for men. Potency disorders, falling hair . . . Later this was played down, but Stella still has the image of being a man's doctor. So there's a very logical explanation for the disproportion."

"Still, the fact remains . . . not a single woman was included among the victims, even though Europe has its share of elderly ladies, too. Does Stella operate any clinics in Europe?"

"No. The European victims never came into contact with Stella. That's pretty safe to assume, since none of them had visited the States within the previous five years."

"Did you ever consider the possibility that there might be two separate operations—one for the Americans, another for the Europeans?"

"We did consider that. We compared both groups within the same set, but nothing came of it."

"Why did he insist on sending his patients to Naples and not somewhere else?"

"Very simple. He's a second-generation Italian, his family comes from somewhere around Naples, and he probably stood to make a profit through his connections with some of the local balneologists, such as Dr. Giono. Medical confidentiality prevented our gaining access to the correspondence, but it's only logical that a doctor on the other side of the ocean would recommend patients to his Italian colleagues. At any rate, we didn't uncover anything suspicious in their relationship. I suppose that for every patient he recommended he received a certain percentage."

"How do you explain that mysterious blank letter delivered after Mittelhorn's death?"

"I suspect it was sent by a member of Mittelhorn's own family, someone who was familiar with the circumstances of his death and who was as eager as Mrs. Barbour to see the investigation continued but who, for one reason or another, couldn't or didn't want to intervene as openly as she did. Someone who had good reason to believe a crime had been committed and was trying to stir up suspicion so the police would keep the case open. The letter was postmarked Switzerland, where Mittelhorn had a number of relatives. . . ."

"Were there any drug addicts among Dr. Stella's patients?"

"Two, neither of them heavy users and both of them elderly men—one a widower, the other a bachelor. Arrived last year around the end of May, beginning of June, took the baths, sunbathed regularly—in short, did everything that according to the statistics should have exposed them to the maximum danger. But the fact is both returned safe and sound. And I shouldn't forget to mention that one was allergic to pollen and the other to strawberries!"

"How disastrous!" exclaimed Barth, but neither of us was in the mood to laugh.

"You figured it was the allergy, didn't you? So did I."

"What kind of drugs were they taking?"

"Marijuana in the case of the one with the strawberry allergy. The one with hay fever was taking LSD, but only once in a while. His supply ran out just before he flew back to the States; that's probably why he quit the baths and left ahead of schedule. In Naples he couldn't get his hands on the stuff. The police had just busted up a huge Middle Eastern ring based in Italy, trafficking had stopped, and the suppliers who hadn't been arrested were lying low."

"And the one with the strawberry allergy..." mumbled Barth. "Well, that takes care of that. What about those with mental problems?"

"Negative. Oh, you know as well as I do there's bound to be something in everyone's family closet, but that would be stretching it too far. All the patients in question—victims as well as survivors—were mentally sound. A few neurotics and insomniacs, but that's about it. Among the men, that is. Among the women patients we found one case of melancholia, one case of depression associated with menopause, and one suicide attempt."

"A suicide attempt, you say?"

"One of those false alarms on the part of a typical neurotic. Poisoned herself under circumstances where she was sure to be saved. With the others it was just the opposite: not one of them had gone around proclaiming a suicidal mania. On the contrary, the repeated attempts give evidence of a ruthless determination."

"Why only in Naples?" Barth asked. "Weren't there any cases reported in places like Messina or Etna?"

"No. Naturally we couldn't check out every sulfur spring in the world, but a special group was assigned to investigate the ones in Italy. An absolute blank. There was a case of someone dying of a shark attack, another in a drowning accident."

"Coburn died in a drowning accident, too, didn't he?"

"Yes, but while temporarily deranged."

"Has that definitely been proved?"

"Almost. We know relatively little about the man. Only that when he was served breakfast that time in his room, he hid his toast, butter, and eggs in an empty cigar box, and later put some food on the window sill before going out."

"Of course! He suspected poison and wanted to see if the birds..."

"And he probably wanted to take the box to a toxicologist but drowned before he had a chance to do so."

"What about the experts' reports?"

"Two thick, typewritten volumes. We even resorted to the Delphi method of polling the experts."

"Well?"

"The majority argued in favor of some unknown psychotropic drug similar in its effect to LSD, though not necessarily having a similar chemical composition."

"An unknown drug? What a strange diagnosis."

"Not necessarily unknown. These same experts believe it might be a combination of several known substances, since the symptoms of a synergy can seldom be deduced from the effects of its individual ingredients."

"What was the minority opinion?"

"An acute psychosis of unknown etiology. You know how loquacious doctors and specialists can be when they're in the dark about something."

"Only too well. Would you mind giving me another rundown based on the typology of cause of death?"

"Not in the least. Coburn died an accidental or premeditated death by drowning. Brunner jumped from a window but survived it—"

"Excuse me, but whatever became of him?"

"He's back in the States, in bad health but still alive. He has a vague recollection of certain things but doesn't like to be reminded of them. All he can remember is having taken a waiter for a member of the Mafia and the feeling of being constantly shadowed. Shall I go on?"

"Please do."

"Osborn was the victim of a hit-and-run accident. The driver of the car has never been found. Emmings twice tried to commit suicide. Died of a self-inflicted gun wound. Leyge, the Swede, drove to Rome and fell from the Colosseum. Schimmelreiter died in the hospital of natural causes, of a lung tumor, after going berserk. Heyne nearly drowned, then slashed his wrists in the hospital. Pulled through but later died of pneumonia. Swift escaped injury. Mittelhorn also tried to commit suicide twice— once with an overdose of sleeping pills, the second time by consuming iodine. Died of internal burns. Titz was killed in a highway accident. Lastly, Adams died in his hotel room at the

Hilton in Rome, apparently from suffocation of unknown cause. The Brigg case is still a mystery."

"Thank you. Of those who escaped alive, do any remember the initial symptoms?"

"Yes. One symptom was a trembling of the hands and a noticeable change in the taste of food. We found that out from Swift. Brunner definitely recalls the food's having an 'off taste' but remembers nothing about any trembling of the hands. His testimony is probably the result of a residual psychic effect. At least that was the opinion of the medical experts."

"The cause of death covers quite a spectrum, and the suicide victims always seemed to resort to whatever means was available at the time. Did you conduct an investigation based on the *cui prodest* principle?"

"You mean did we investigate those who stood to gain financially? That would have been pointless, since there was nothing in the way of evidence to connect any of the heirs with the individual deaths."

"Any press coverage?"

"A total news blackout. Of course the local papers ran obituaries on each of the fatalities, but these got lost among all the other accident reports. We were worried they might interfere with the investigation. Only one paper in the States, the name of which escapes me, made any mention of the tragic fates met by the patients of Dr. Stella. Stella himself insisted it was the work of some unscrupulous competitor. Even so, last year he didn't send a single patient to Naples."

"So he stopped! Doesn't that look suspicious?"

"Not necessarily. One more incident and the publicity could have cost him more than he stood to make on the deal. He couldn't have been making very much on the kickbacks."

"I now propose we play the following game," suggested Barth. "We'll call it 'How to die a mysterious death in Naples.' The purpose of the game will be to find out how one qualifies for such a death. Will you help me out?"

"By all means. The list of qualifications will include a person's sex, age, build, physical disabilities, financial status, plus some other characteristics that I'll try to specify. To qualify one would have to be a male in his fifties, rather tall, the athletic or the pyknic type, a bachelor, a widower, or divorced, but in any case single during the time spent in Naples. As is evident from the Schimmelreiter case, financial prosperity is not an absolute requirement. Nor should one know any Italian, or if so, only a smattering."

"None of the victims was fluent in Italian?"

"Not one. Now for the more specific characteristics. To be a candidate one should not be a diabetic."

"Is that so?"

"There wasn't a single diabetic in the whole series. On the other hand, there were five known diabetics among the rheumatic patients sent to Naples by Dr. Stella, all of whom returned home safely."

"How do your experts explain that?"

"I'm not really sure I can answer that. Some ascribed it to the patient's metabolism, to the formation of acetone derivatives that might possibly have acted as an antidote, though this was challenged by some of the less distinguished—but in my opinion more honest—experts. Acetone derivatives form in the blood when an organism begins to suffer the effects of an insulin deficiency. But nowadays every diabetic is warned to take his prescribed medicine regularly. The next requirement is an allergy. Hypersensitivity to grass, hay fever, asthma. But then there were people who met all of the above conditions and still managed to escape unharmed. Take the patient with the strawberry allergy, or the one with hay fever."

"Single, well-to-do men who took the mineral baths, were athletic in build, suffered from an allergy, and didn't know Italian?"

"They even used the same antihistamines as the others, in addition to Plimasine."

"What's that?"

"An antihistamine with the added ingredient Ritalin. Ritalin is α-phenyl-α-piperidineacetic acid methyl ester hydrochloride. The first substance in Plimasine, Pyribenzamine, neutralizes the symptoms of allergic reaction but causes drowsiness and a diminution of the reflexes. That's why drivers are advised to take it in combination with Ritalin, which is classified as a stimulant."

"You're quite a chemist, I see!"

"I've been taking Plimasine for years. Anyone who has an allergy is to some extent his own doctor. In the States I used to take an equivalent medication, since Plimasine is manufactured in Switzerland. Charles Decker, the man with the hay fever, was also on Plimasine, yet no one touched a hair on his head— Wait a moment."

I sat there with gaping mouth like a moron. Barth stared at me in silence.

"They all showed signs of baldness," I said at last.

"Baldness?"

"The beginning stages, at least. Wait a minute. Right, Decker had a bald spot, too . . . at the back of the head. But that still doesn't . . . oh, never mind."

"But you're not exactly bald," observed Barth.

"Sorry? Oh, right—I'm not. That was an oversight. But if Decker escaped injury . . . even though he showed signs of baldness . . . But what connection could there be between baldness and insanity?"

"Or between insanity and diabetes?"

"You're right, doctor, that's not a valid question."

"Was the question of baldness completely overlooked?"

"The situation was like this. We compared those who died with those who left Naples unharmed. The question of baldness certainly came up. The problem was that verification was possible only in the case of the victims, since most of the survivors would have been reluctant to admit they were wearing a toupee. Human pride being what it is, this is one area where people tend to be extremely sensitive, and getting people to submit willingly to an on-the-spot examination would have been tricky. Also, it would have meant trying to locate the place where the wig or hair transplant had been ordered, and we simply had neither the time nor the staff for that."

"Wasn't it considered very relevant?"

"People were divided. Some thought it was a waste of time trying to establish whether any of the survivors was anxious to conceal his baldness, and didn't see what connection that would have with the tragic fates of the others."

"Well, then, if you had taken the hair factor into consideration, why did you act so startled a moment ago?"

"It was a negative correlation, I'm afraid. What startled me was that none of the deceased had tried to conceal his baldness. Not one of them had worn a toupee or undergone a hair transplant. There are such operations, you know."

"So I've heard. Anything else?"

"Nothing—except that all the victims were in the process of going bald and made no effort to conceal it, whereas the survivors included both those who were balding and those with a normal head of hair. A minute ago I was reminded of Decker's bald spot, that's all. For a moment I thought I'd stumbled onto something. It wouldn't have been the first time, either. You see, I've been at this for so long that now and then I begin seeing things, phantoms. . . ."

"Oh, that smacks of magic spells, spirits from the other world. . . . But maybe there's something to it."

"Do you believe in the existence of spirits?" A long and hard stare.

"It's probably enough if *they* believed in them, isn't it? Let's suppose some fortuneteller was operating in Naples, someone who went after rich foreign clients. . . ."

"All right. Supposing there was such a person," I said, sitting up in my chair, "what then?"

"Let's assume this fortuneteller tries to win people's confidence through various kinds of tricks and séances, gives away samples of some miraculous elixir imported from Tibet, some type of narcotic that makes the client totally dependent on him or is passed off as a cure-all for every conceivable ailment. . . .

Now let's suppose that out of a hundred such cases there are some ten or eleven who rashly consume an overdose of the stuff. . . ."

"Right!" I exclaimed. "But in that case wouldn't the Italians have been wise to his little game? The Italian police, I mean? The fact is that in some cases we were so familiar with the victim's routine we knew exactly when he left the hotel, what he liked to wear, which were his favorite newsstands and even which papers he bought, which cabin he used for changing clothes at the beach, what and where he ate, which opera performances he saw. . . . Now we might have missed such a quack or guru in one or two instances, but not in every single case. No, there never was any such person. Besides, the whole thing sounds too far-fetched. It's not just that none of them knew Italian; but would a Swede with a university education, a rare-book dealer, and a respectable businessman be likely to visit an Italian fortuneteller? Besides, none of them would have had the time. . . ."

"Refuted but not defeated. Here goes another wild shot." He sat up in his chair. "If something had them hooked, then it must have strung them along gently and without leaving a trace. Right?"

"Right."

"No what else could have hooked them in a purely private, intimate, and casual sort of way but—sex!"

I hesitated before answering.

"No. Granted, there were a few brief erotic encounters, but that's hardly the same thing. Believe me, we did such a thorough background check we couldn't possibly have overlooked anything as 'big' as a woman, a sex orgy, or a brothel. No, it must have been something else, something utterly banal. . . ."

I was a little surprised by these last words of mine, since I'd never thought of it in such terms before. But it turned out to be grist for Barth's mill.

"Banal but lethal . . . Yes, why not! Some shameful and hidden desire, some secret lust that had to be satisfied . . . Not shameful to us, perhaps, but something that might have meant a horrible scandal for others if it were ever made public . . ."

"The circle has closed," I said. "Because now you've come around to the very same position you forced me to abandon a while ago, namely, psychology. . . ."

Someone honked outside. Looking very young at that moment, the doctor stood up, peered down below, and shook his finger threateningly. The honking stopped. I was surprised to notice it had already grown dark. I consulted my watch and was shocked to discover that I'd taken up three hours of Barth's time. I stood up to say good-bye, but he refused to hear anything of the sort.

"Oh, no, you don't. First of all, you'll stay with us for dinner. Second, we didn't settle anything. And third, or, rather, first and foremost, I'd like to apologize for reversing the roles and grilling you like some examining magistrate. I'll admit I had an ulterior motive, one not exactly worthy of a host. . . . I wanted to find out certain things—both about you and from you— things I couldn't get from the files. It's always been my feeling that only a person can convey the atmosphere of a case. At times I was even out to provoke you a little, to needle you, but I must say you took it very well, though you haven't nearly as good a poker face as you imagine you do. . . . If there's anything that can redeem me in your eyes, then let it be my good intentions, because I'm ready to offer you my services. But let's sit down until dinner's served. They'll ring when it's ready."

We sat down again. I felt enormously relieved.

"I'll work on the case," he continued, "though I don't believe we'll have much luck. . . . May I ask exactly how you envision my role?"

"This is a case lending itself to a multifactorial analysis," I began cautiously, selecting my words with care. "I'm not familiar with your program but I am familiar with a number of GPSS-type programs, and I assume your computer is somewhat analogous. The problem is not so much a criminal as an intellectual one. Obviously the computer won't be able to identify the culprit, but it might be able to eliminate the culprit as an unknown factor. Solving the case would mean positing a theory to account for the fatalities, a law governing these deaths. . . ."

Dr. Barth looked at me almost with sympathy. Or perhaps is was only the way the light fell from above, gently modulating his features every time he made the slightest movement.

"When I said *we* I had in mind a team of men, not electrons. I've assembled a brilliant interdisciplinary team, including some of the best minds of France, and I'm sure they'd jump at the chance. . . . But as for the computer . . . True, we've managed to program one, and so far the test results have been satisfactory, but with such a case—never. . . ." He shook his head.

"Why not?"

"Very simple. The computer won't work without hard data." He spread out his arms. "And what are we supposed to use as hard data in this case? Let's suppose a new narcotics ring is operating in Naples, that a hotel is being used as a drop, and they are delivering the stuff by substituting it for the salt in certain salt shakers. Now isn't it possible for the salt shakers to get switched around occasionally on the dining-room tables? In that case wouldn't only those who like salt on their food run the risk of getting drugged? And how, may I ask, is a computer supposed to process this if the processing data include nothing about the salt shakers, the drugs, or the culinary habits of the victims?"

I looked at him with admiration. How adept he was at manipulating such ideas. The dinner bell rang, louder and louder till it reached a shrill intensity, then suddenly stopped, and a woman's voice could be heard scolding a child.

"It's time for us to go downstairs. . . . We always eat on schedule."

The dining room was lit by a long row of pink candles on the table. On the way down Barth whispered that his grandmother would be joining them for dinner, adding that for a ninety-year-old woman she was still extremely fit, if a little on the eccentric side. I took this as a warning of sorts, but before I had a chance to reply I found myself being introduced to the other members of the family. Besides the three children whom I'd already met, and Mrs. Barth, who was already seated across the table in a hand-carved chair identical to the one in the library, I saw an elderly lady dressed in a gown of royal purple. An old-fashioned lorgnette trimmed with diamonds glittered on her chest, and her small black eyes transfixed me like a couple of shiny pebbles. She held out her hand, but so high and with such enthusiasm that I kissed it, something I otherwise never do; and in a surprisingly deep and masculine voice, one that sounded as false as a voice in a poorly dubbed film, she said:

"So you're an astronaut, are you? I've never sat at the same table with an astronaut before."

Even the doctor was taken by surprise. Mrs. Barth was quick to remark that the children had announced my arrival. The old lady told me to sit down next to her and to speak in a loud voice, as she was hard of hearing. Next to her table setting was a kidney-shaped hearing aid, but at no time during the meal did she use it.

"You can keep me entertained," she said. "I doubt whether I shall have a similar occasion so soon again. Please, be so kind as to tell me how the earth *really* looks from up there? I don't trust the photographs."

"And rightly so," I said, passing her the salad bowl, secretly charmed by her blunt and unceremonious manner. "No photo can ever match it, especially not when the orbital path is close and the earth gradually takes the place of the sky. It doesn't block the sky, it *becomes* the sky. That's the impression one gets."

"Is it really as beautiful as they say?" Her voice expressed doubt.

"It was to me, anyhow. What impressed me most was the emptiness of it, the desolation. Not a sign of any cities, highways, or seaports—nothing but oceans, continents, and clouds. By the way, the oceans and continents look much the same as we were taught at school. But the clouds ... I found the clouds to be the most uncanny thing of all, maybe because they didn't look like clouds."

"What *did* they look like?"

"That depends on the altitude. From very far away they look like the old and wrinkly hide of a rhinoceros, all cracked and bluish-gray. But the closer you get, the more they look like different shades of sheep's wool after it's been combed out."

"Were you ever on the moon?"

"I'm sorry to say I never was."

I was preparing myself for more questions of a cosmological nature when she abruptly changed the subject.

"You speak French so fluently, but with a strange accent and a slightly different vocabulary. You're not from Canada, are you?"

"My family was Canadian; I was born in the States."

"Just as I thought: Then your mother is French?"

"*Was* French."

I could see that both husband and wife were trying to dampen the old lady's curiosity by means of glances from across the table, but she simply ignored them.

"And did your mother speak French with you?"

"Yes, she did."

"Your first name is John. So she must have called you Jean."

"She did."

"Then I shall call you that. Please take away the asparagus, Jean—I'm not supposed to eat it. The secret of growing old, Jean, is having lots of experience you can no longer use. They're right"—she said, indicating the rest of the family—"not to pay me any attention. You're still too young to know, but there's quite a difference between being seventy and being ninety. A *fundamental* difference," she added for emphasis. She stopped talking and began eating her meal, and came to life again only when the table was being cleared in preparation for the next course.

"How many times did you travel to outer space?"

"Twice. But I didn't travel very far from earth. If you compare it to an apple, then only as far as the peel is thick."

"Aren't you being modest?"

"Not really."

The conversation had taken a somewhat strange turn, but I can't say I found it awkward, especially since the old lady had a special charm about her. And so I was not the least bit irritated when she went on with her interrogation.

"Are you in favor of letting women travel in outer space?"

"I really haven't given it much thought," I answered honestly. "If that's their ambition, then why not?"

"You're the ones who started that whole crazy movement, aren't you? That women's liberation business. It's so childish, so tasteless, though it certainly is convenient."

"Do you think so? Why convenient?"

"It's always convenient to know who's to blame for everything. Everything's the fault of men, say the ladies. They're the only ones who can straighten out the world. They want to take your place. As preposterous as it may sound, they do have a definite goal in mind, which is more than can be said of you men."

After a dessert of rhubarb sprinkled with sugar, the kids sneaked out of the dining room and I got ready to leave. But when the doctor heard I was staying at Orly, he insisted I move in with him. I had no desire to take advantage of him, but I was sorely tempted. To put it bluntly, I wanted to pester the hell out of him.

Mrs. Barth seconded her husband's invitation and showed me their still-empty guest book, saying it would bring good luck if an astronaut were the first to sign it. After a round or two of polite exchanges, I finally gave in. It was decided that I would move in with them the following day. Dr. Barth accompanied me to my car and after I was behind the wheel confided that his grandmother had taken a distinct liking to me, adding that this was no small honor. He was still standing in the gateway as I drove off and plunged into a Parisian night.

To avoid the traffic I swung around the center of the city and headed for the boulevards along the Seine, where the midnight traffic was sure to be lighter. I was tired but contented. My conversation with Barth had left me feeling extremely hopeful. I took it easy on the road, not trusting myself after drinking all that white wine. Ahead of me a small 2 CV was nervously hugging the curb. The road was deserted. Warehouses loomed high above the railings that ran along the opposite bank of the Seine, but I hardly noticed them: my mind was wandering. Suddenly a pair of car lights blazed in the rear-view mirror like a couple of suns. I was right in the middle of passing the 2 CV and was a little too far over to the left, so I decided to make way for the night racer and drop back into the slow lane, but it was too late. His headlights flooded the inside of my car, and a second later a flattened-out shape came shooting through the gap. By the time I recovered from the air blast, he was gone. Something was missing from the right front fender. All that was left of the mirror was the stem. Cut off. A little farther down the road it occurred to me that if it hadn't been for the wine I would have blocked its path and might now be lying underneath the wreckage of my own car. Now *that* would have given Randy food for thought. How beautifully my death would have fit the Naples pattern. How sure Randy would have been it was connected with the simulation mission. But it seems I wasn't fated to be the twelfth victim: I made it back to the hotel safely.

* * *

On the fourth day of my visit, on a Sunday, in order to put his team's involvement in the case on a more personal basis, and also perhaps to show off his new house, Barth held a little get-together at his place to which more than twenty people were invited. Since I hadn't been prepared for any formal affairs, I decided to drive to Paris on Saturday to pick up something more appropriate for the occasion, but Barth talked me out of it. So, dressed as I was in a pair of faded jeans and a scraggly sweater—all my better clothes had been ruined by the Italian police—I stood at the entrance along with the Barths. The walls on the ground floor had been opened up, converting the downstairs area into a spacious drawing room. It was a rather strange situation: surrounded by a crowd of bearded neophytes and periwigged bluestockings, I felt a little like a crasher and a little like a host, inasmuch as I was Barth's houseguest and was even sharing the honors of the house. Being neatly trimmed and shaven, I must have made the impression of an overaged Boy Scout.

Curiously absent from the party was that atmosphere of courtly formality, or even worse that revolutionary clowning so characteristic of intellectuals: ever since the latest events in China, the Maoists had gone into hiding. I made an effort to socialize with all the guests because I knew they had come expressly to meet an allergic astronaut, a roaming detective ad interim. Nonchalantly the conversation turned to the tribulations of the world. Not nonchalantly, really, but in a mood of surrender now that Europe's eternal mission had come to an end, a fact that these graduates of Nanterre and l'École Supérieure seemed to grasp better than their compatriots. Europe had survived, but only in an economic sense. Prosperity had been restored, but not the feeling of self-confidence. It was not the cancer patient's fear of malignancy, but the awareness that the spirit of history had moved on, and that if it ever returned it would not be here. France had lost its power and influence, and now that it had been moved from the stage into the audience it was at liberty to show concern for the sufferings of the world. McLuhan's prophecies were coming true, but in an inverse sort of way, as prophecies have a habit of doing. His "global village" was already here, but split into two halves. The poorer half was suffering, while the wealthier half was importing that suffering via television and commiserating from a distance. That it couldn't go on like this was everywhere taken for granted, but it went on just the same. No one asked for my opinion on the State Department's new "wait and see" policy within the economic buffer zone, nor did I venture to offer any.

The conversation then switched from the trials of the world to its follies. Among other things, I learned that a famous French film director was planning to make a film about the "massacre on the steps." The part of the mysterious hero was to be played by Jean-Paul Belmondo; the little girl would be played not by a child actress—since bedding down with a kid would have been considered in bad taste—but by a famous British movie star. Being just recently married, this same actress had invited a number of prominent personalities to her public wedding night—such pastimes were now the vogue—in order to take up a collection around the nuptial bed for the benefit of the airport casualties in Rome. Ever since reading about those Belgian nuns who indulged in charitable prostitution in order to redeem the hypocrisy of the Church, I'm no longer appalled by such things. And of course there was a lot of talk about politics. The latest news item was that members of an Argentine movement of national patriots had been exposed as government stooges. Various people expressed the fear that something like that couldn't be ruled out even in a country like France. Fascism had survived, along with the most ruthless dictatorships— at least in Europe—whereas the only way to deal effectively with extremist terror was to exterminate the activists. Although a democracy refused to condone "preventive murders," it nonetheless looked the other way when it came to progovernment assassinations carried out under discreet supervision and with limited liability. This was not to be confused with the old-fashioned type of political execution or repression instituted by the State, but was, rather, a form of constructive terror *per procurationem*. I once heard of a philosophy that advocated the total legalization of violence, which even de Sade regarded as the epitome of true freedom. It would have constitutionally sanctioned every sort of activity—revolutionary as well as reactionary; and since the supporters of the *status quo* far outnumbered the subversives, the established order was sure to emerge intact in a violent confrontation of both extremes, should it ever come to something like a civil war.

Around eleven Barth began showing the more curious guests around the house, leaving only a handful of people downstairs. I decided to join three of the guests who were sitting around an open patio door. Two were mathematicians belonging to rival camps: Saussure, a relative of Lagrange, was specializing in analysis, that is, in pure mathematics; the other was in applied mathematics, being a programmer and statistician by profession. Even their outward appearance offered an amusing contrast. Saussure looked as if he might have stepped out of a daguerreotype—lean, dark-haired, with chiseled features, bushy sideburns, a gold pince-nez dangling on a ribbon—and wore a Japanese transistorized calculator around his neck like a medal, which was obviously meant as a joke. The statistician, a burly, curly-headed blond, was a double for the slouchy Boche featured in French postcards from the time of the First World War, and was in fact of German origin. His name was Mayer, and not Mailleux, as I thought at first after hearing it pronounced that way. The mathematicians were in no hurry to make conversation, unlike the third man, a pharmacologist named Dr. Lapidus. Sporting a full-length beard, he looked as if he'd just returned from an uninhabited island. He asked me whether the investigation had turned up any abortive cases, that is, cases where the outward signs of insanity had simply come and gone. I answered that all the files were on microfilm, and that unless one wanted to classify the Swift case as abortive, there were none falling into that category.

"That's amazing!" he exclaimed.

"Why amazing?"

"The symptoms varied in their intensity, but the moment any of the victims was hospitalized, like that man who jumped out the window, they immediately subsided. If one assumes the psychosis was chemically induced, that would mean the dose taken had a strange kind of cumulative effect. Didn't anyone notice this?"

"I don't really see your point."

"There's no psychotropic compound known to have such a

delayed effect that, say, if it were taken on Monday it could begin producing the first symptoms on Tuesday, cause hallucinations on Wednesday, and reach a maximum intensity on Saturday. Of course it might be possible to build up a supply by using a hypodermic injection that it would take several weeks to absorb; but such a procedure would leave traces in the body, and I found nothing in the autopsy reports to indicate this."

"You didn't find anything because nothing like that was ever reported."

"That's what I find amazing!"

"But they might have taken the stuff more than once, which would explain the cumulative effect. . . ."

He shook his head with disapproval.

"How? Between the change in routine and the appearance of the first symptoms there was always a time lapse of six to eight days on the average, nine in one case. And no chemical agent is capable of having such a delayed or cumulative effect. Let's assume they started taking this chemical substance the first or second day after their arrival; then the initial symptoms would have had to occur within the next forty-eight hours. In the case of patients with kidney or liver diseases that's debatable, but then there weren't any such patients."

"So what's your opinion?"

"The case histories would indicate they were drugged on a *steady, gradual,* and *continual* basis."

"So you believe it was a case of premeditated poisoning?"

He broke out in a smile, revealing his gold teeth.

"No. Who knows, maybe the goblins are to blame, or maybe some flies were on their way back from raiding a pharmaceutical lab and happened to land on the victims' toast after tramping around in the latest derivatives of lysergic acid. But I do know that the process of accretion took place *gradually.*"

"But what if it were an unknown compound?"

"Unknown to *us?*"

He said it in such a way that I couldn't help smiling.

"Yes. Unknown to you. To chemistry. Would that be impossible?"

He made a wry grimace and flashed the gold in his mouth.

"There are more unknown compounds than there are stars in the sky. But you can't have any that are both resistant and nonresistant to tissue metabolism. There are many circles, but there is no such thing as a squared circle."

"I don't follow you."

"Very simple. Chemical agents known to cause acute reactions act by binding irreversibly to the body's hemoglobin to form insoluble compounds with carbon monoxide or cyanide. An autopsy will always be able to detect the presence of such agents, especially if micromethods are used—chromatography, for example. But even with the help of chromatography they couldn't find any traces! That means the chemical agent involved must be easily degradable. If it's easily degradable, then it would have to be administered in a number of small doses or else in one massive dose. But if it were administered in a single dose, then the symptoms would start becoming noticeable in a matter of hours and not days. Now do you follow me?"

"Yes. Do you see any other possibilities?"

"There is one other. And that is if it involved some basically innocuous substance that began developing psychotropic properties the moment it started distributing itself in the blood or tissue. In the liver, for instance. To expel this substance the liver might convert it into a toxic agent. The result would be an interesting biochemical trap, though a completely hypothetical one, since nothing like that has ever been known to happen and I doubt whether it ever could."

"How can you be so sure?"

"Because pharmacology has no record of such a toxin, of such a 'Trojan horse.' And if something has never been known to happen, the chances are slim that it ever will."

"So where does that leave us?"

"I don't know."

"Is *that* all you have to say?"

I was being impolite, but the man was beginning to get on my nerves. Even so, he didn't seem to take offense.

"No, that's not all. The effect could be the result of something else."

"A combination of different substances? Of different toxins?"

"Yes."

"But that would definitely make it a case of premeditated murder, wouldn't it?"

The answer came unexpectedly from Saussure.

"A girl from Lombardy was working as a housemaid for a certain Parisian lawyer living at 48 Rue St-Pierre, on the third floor. One day her sister came to visit her but forgot the name of the street, confusing it with St-Michel. When she came to 48 Boulevard St-Michel, she went unstairs, found a doctor's nameplate, rang the doorbell, and asked for her sister, Maria Duval. By sheer coincidence it turned out that a woman with the exact same name—Maria Duval—was working for another doctor, on another street, but was in fact somebody else entirely. Now in trying to determine the a priori probability of such a coincidence, we find it impossible to offer a rational, that is to say, mathematically valid explanation. The example may appear trivial, but, believe me, it opens up an endless void. The only model for the theory of probability is Gibbs's world of recurrent events. When it comes to unique and statistically unclassifiable events, the theory of probability is inapplicable."

"There are no such things as unique events," said Mayer, who all this time had been standing there in amusement, grinning wryly.

"Of course there are," countered Saussure.

"At least not as a set."

"You happen to be a unique set of events yourself. Everyone is."

"Distributively or collectively speaking?"

Just when it looked as if we were in for a duel of abstractions, Lapidus placed a hand on each man's knee and said:

"Gentlemen!"

Both men smiled. Mayer went on smirking with tongue in cheek while Saussure tried to pick up where he had left off.

"One can easily run a frequency analysis on the name Duval or the residences of Parisian doctors. But what's the ratio between confusing Rue St-Pierre with Boulevard St-Michel, and the frequency of these names as street names throughout France? And what numerical value do you assign to a situation in which the woman finds a house with an occupant named Duval but on the fourth, rather than the third floor? In short, the set of possibilities is limitless."

"But not infinite," interjected Mayer.

"I can prove it's infinite in both the classical and the transfinite sense."

"Excuse me," I interrupted, wishing to pick up the thread. "Dr. Saussure, I'm sure your story had a moral to it. What exactly was the moral?"

Mayer gave me a sympathetic glance and strode out onto the patio. Saussure seemed somewhat startled by my lack of perspicacity.

"Have you been out in the garden behind the summerhouse, out where the strawberry patch is?"

"Why, yes."

"Did you happen to notice the round wooden table standing there, the one trimmed with copper nails?"

"Yes."

"Do you think it would be possible to take an eyedropper and squeeze out as many drops as there are nails so that each drop hits a nail head?"

"Well . . . if a person were to take careful aim, why not?"

"But not if a person just started firing away at random?"

"Then obviously not."

"But five minutes of a steady downpour and each nail would be *sure* to get hit by a drop of water."

"You mean to say . . ." I was beginning to see his point.

"Yes, yes! My position is an extreme one: there's no such

- 125 -

thing as a mysterious event. It all depends on the magnitude of the set. The greater the set, the greater the chance of improbable events occurring within it."

"Then the victims do not really form a set . . . ?"

"The victims were the result of a random causality. Out of that realm of infinite possibilities I mentioned earlier, you chose a certain fraction of cases that exhibited a multifactorial similarity. You then treated these as an entire set, and that's why they seem mysterious."

"So you would agree with Mr. Lapidus that we should investigate the abortive cases?"

"No. For the simple reason that they would be impossible to find. The class of soldiers stationed at the front includes the subclass of both killed and wounded. While these two groups can be differentiated easily, you'll never be able to differentiate those soldiers who came within an inch of being hit from those who missed being hit by a kilometer. That's why you'll never find out anything except by sheer accident. An adversary who relies on a strategy of chance can only be defeated by the same strategy."

"Are you at it again, Dr. Saussure?" came a voice from behind us. It was Barth, accompanied by a lean, grizzly-haired man whose name I failed to catch when we were introduced. Barth treated Saussure not as a member of his team but more as a curiosity. I later found out that until a year ago Saussure had been working for Futuribles before joining up with the French CETI investigating the possibility of extraterrestrial civilizations, but that he had always been something of a drifter. I asked him whether he believed such civilizations existed.

"That's not so simple," he said, rising to his feet. "Other civilizations exist and at the same time do not exist."

"Meaning?"

"They do not exist as projections of our own concept of civilization, from which it follows that man is incapable of defining what makes these civilizations be civilizations."

"Perhaps," I conceded. "Still, it must be possible to define our place in the cosmos, don't you think? Either we're nothing but a drab mediocrity, or we're an exception, and a glaring one at that."

Our listeners broke out laughing, and I was surprised to learn that it was precisely this line of reasoning that had persuaded Saussure to quit the CETI. At the moment he was the only one not laughing; he just stood there, fingering his calculator as if it were a pendant. After luring him away from the others and maneuvering him over to the table, I offered him a glass of wine, poured myself one, and, while drinking to his version of civilization, asked him to share his views with me.

This was a shrewd tactic, one I'd learned from Fitzpatrick: affecting an air of seriousness bordering on parody. Saussure began by explaining that the progress of human knowledge was a gradual renunciation of the *simplicity* of the world. "Man wanted everything to be simple, even if mysterious: one God— in the singular, of course; one form of natural law; one principle of reason in the universe, and so on. Astronomy, for example, held that the totality of existence was made up of stars—past, present, and future—and their debris in the form of planets. But gradually astronomy had to concede that a number of cosmic phenomena couldn't be contained within its scheme of things. Man's hunger for simplicity paved the way for Ockham's razor, the principle stating that no entity, no category can be multiplied unnecessarily. But the complexity that we refused to acknowledge finally overcame our prejudices. Modern physics has turned Ockham's maxim upside down by positing that everything is possible. Everything in physics, that is; the complexity of civilizations is far greater than that of physics."

I could have gone on listening to him, but just then Lapidus insisted on introducing me to a group of doctors and biologists. All were of the same opinion: not enough data. The consensus was that one should start with the hypothesis that the deaths were caused by a congenitally determined reaction to certain unknown elements in the microbiosphere. Two groups should be singled out for study—forty in each, all men in their fifties,

all having an athletic or a pyknic build, all randomly selected—
and made to undergo a steady program of sulfur baths, sun-
bathing, body massages, sudorifics, ultraviolet lamps, horror
films, and some titillating pornography, until one of them
showed signs of cracking. A genealogical study would then have
to be made of their hereditary backgrounds for any sudden or
unexplained deaths, which is where the computer would come
in handy. They had gone on to discuss the chemical composition of the bathing water and the air, the subject of adreno-
chromes, the possibility of a chemogenic schizophrenia of
metabolic origin—when Dr. Barth came to my rescue and began
introducing me to the legal experts on the team. Some of the
lawyers argued in favor of the Mafia, others in favor of some
new and hitherto undisclosed organization that was in no
hurry to claim responsibility for the mysterious deaths. Their
motive? But, then, what motive did that Japanese have for
slaughtering all those Serbs, Dutchmen, and Germans in
Rome? And had I seen today's papers? A New Zealand tourist
had tried to protest the kidnapping of an Australian diplomat in
Bolivia by hijacking a charter plane in Helsinki that was carrying pilgrims bound for the Vatican. That principle of Roman
law which said "*id fecit cui prodest*" was no longer valid. No,
it had to be the Mafia, since any one of the Italians could have
been a mafioso: the street vendor, the hotel porter, the bath
attendant, the taxicab driver. . . . And the acute psychosis would
suggest the presence of hallucinogens; although slipping someone a hallucinogen in a restaurant might have been tricky,
where else would a person be apt to gulp down a cool, refresh-
ing drink if not in a health spa after a hot and sweaty bath? The
lawyers were then surrounded by the doctors, whose company
I had just left, and an argument broke out on the subject of
baldness, but without resolving anything. The whole scene was
rather comical. Around one o'clock the smaller groups began
merging to form a fairly animated crowd, and while champagne
was being served the subject of sex came up. All were convinced that the list of drugs and medications found on the vic-

tims was incomplete. Why was that? Because it didn't include any of the latest sex stimulants or aphrodisiacs, and you could be sure the older men were using them. Topcraft, Bios 6, Dulong, Antipraecox, Orkasfluid, Sex Tonicum, Sanurex Erecta, Elixire d'Égypte, Erectovite, Topform, Action Cream—the market was flooded with them. I was overwhelmed by this display of erudition, and also a little embarrassed, since they'd managed to reveal a flaw in the investigation: at no time had anyone bothered to investigate the psychotropic effects of such medications. I was advised to look into it. You mean to say that not one of these medications was found on the victims? That in itself was suspicious. A younger man wouldn't make any bones about it, but then we all know how older men are apt to be secretive, prudish, and self-conscious when it comes to such matters. They had probably used the stuff and got rid of the wrappers. . . .

The party was getting noisy; windows were thrown open; corks went flying; a smiling Barth kept popping in and out of different doorways; Spanish girls made the rounds with trays; a platinum blonde—Lapidus's wife, I guessed—not bad-looking in the dark, said I reminded her of an ex-boyfriend. . . . The party was a grand success. And yet I was in such a blue, melancholic mood, mellowed by the champagne: I felt cheated. Not one of these rather amiable hotshots had any of that flair, that special flash of illumination which in art went by the name of inspiration, that ability to sniff out what's relevant from a pile of facts. They didn't care about finding a solution to the problem; they only wanted to complicate it by inventing new ones. Randy had the gift but was short on the sort of erudition of which the Barth house was chock full—full but unfired.

I stuck around till the very end, joined my hosts in seeing off the last of the guests, watched as car after car went down the driveway till it was empty, gazed up at the house ablaze with lights, then went upstairs feeling defeated and disaffected. More with myself than with anyone else. Outside, a refulgent Paris loomed beyond the dark stretch of gardens and suburban clutter, but its refulgence was not enough to eclipse the planet Mars, now radiantly ascendant above the horizon: a yellow sphere someone had put there as the final dot.

✳   ✳   ✳

There are friends with whom we share neither interests nor any particular experiences, friends with whom we never correspond, whom we seldom meet and then only by chance, but whose existence nonetheless has for us a special if uncanny meaning. For me the Eiffel Tower is just such a friend, and not merely because it happens to be the symbol of a city, for Paris leaves me neither hot nor cold. I first became aware of this attachment of mine when reading in the paper about plans for its demolition, the mere thought of which filled me with alarm.

Whenever I'm in Paris I make a point of going to see it. To look and see, that's all. Toward the end of my visit I like to step under its foundation, to station myself between its four iron pylons and gaze up at its interlacing arches, the intricate trusswork outlined against the sky, and the grand, old-fashioned wheels used to propel the elevator. The day after the get-together at Barth's was no exception. Though it was now completely hemmed in by high-rise boxes, the tower was just as impressive as ever.

It was a bright and sunny day. Sitting on a bench, I thought about how I might back out of the whole affair—I'd already made up my mind the moment I woke up that morning. After all that effort, the mission now seemed to me so phony and irrelevant and misguided. Especially misguided was my enthusiasm. It was like a moment of self-revelation: behind all the major decisions in my life I saw the same impulsiveness, the same infantile thinking. On impulse I had enlisted in the commandos as an eighteen-year-old and wound up a spectator of the Normandy invasion—from a stretcher, that is; my glider, after taking enemy flak, had crash-landed off target, with me and a crew of thirty on board, right on top of some German bunkers, and the next day I found myself in an English field

- 130 -

hospital with a broken tailbone. Mars was just a repeat performance. Even if I'd made it up there and back I couldn't have gone on reminiscing about it forever; otherwise I might have gone the route of that astronaut who wound up contemplating suicide because everything else seemed so anticlimactic by comparison, including offers to sit on the board of directors of several large corporations. One of my fellow astronauts had been made managing director of a Florida beer-distributing company; and now, every time I reach for a can of beer, I always see him stepping into the elevator in his angel-white spacesuit. That's why I'd joined the Naples mission: I had no intention of following in their footsteps.

Now, as I stood looking up at the Eiffel Tower, it all seemed so clear to me. It was a frustrating profession, so tempting with its promise of that "big step for mankind" which was, at the same time, in Armstrong's words, a "small step for man"; but in reality it was a high point, an apogee (and not only in the astronomical sense); a position in danger of being lost, a symbolic image of human life in which the lust for the unattainable consumes all of man's powers and hopes. Only up there hours take the place of years, and a man's best years at that. Aldrin knew that the prints left by his space boots would survive not only the Apollo program but mankind as well, that they would be eroded only when the sun expanded into the earth's orbit one and a half billion years from now. So how could a man who'd been so close to eternity settle for a beer distributor's job? To know that from then on it was all downhill, and to have experienced it in such an intense and irrevocable manner, that's more than a letdown; that's a mockery. As I sat there admiring this iron monument erected to the last century by a master engineer, I wondered even more at my own fanaticism, at my own stubborn persistence, and it was now only a feeling of shame that kept me from racing back to Garges and packing my things on the sly. Shame and a sense of loyalty.

That afternoon Barth dropped by my guestroom in the attic. He seemed a little on edge. News. Inspector Pingaud, the

Sûreté's liaison with the Barth team, had invited both of us to his office. To brief us about a past investigation headed by one of Pingaud's colleagues, Superintendent Leclerc. Pingaud felt that the case merited our attention. Naturally I agreed to the interview, and we drove off to Paris together.

Pingaud was expecting us. The moment I saw him I recognized him as the quiet, gray-haired man I'd seen at Barth's side the night before, though he was much older than I'd taken him to be. He greeted us in a little side room, and as he stood up I noticed a tape recorder lying on his desk. Dispensing with any preliminaries, he told us the superintendent had been to see him the day before yesterday—though retired, the superintendent was in the habit of dropping in on old friends. During their conversation Leclerc had made reference to a case that he couldn't brief me on personally but that the inspector persuaded him to record on tape. Because it was a rather lengthy story, he invited us to make ourselves comfortable, then left us alone in the room. He did this seemingly as a matter of courtesy, not wishing to disturb us perhaps, but the whole thing struck me as fishy.

I wasn't accustomed to police hospitality, much less from the French police. Then again, maybe it was too little. Not that I detected any outright discrepancies in Pingaud's version; I had no reason to believe it was a fake investigation or that the superintendent wasn't really retired. Still, nothing would have been easier than to set up a private meeting somewhere. I could understand it if they were reluctant to drag out the files —the files being something sacrosanct for these people—but the tape recorder alone implied they were anxious to avoid any sort of discussion. The briefing was to take place without commentary: you can't very well pump a tape recorder. But why the elaborate cover? Barth was either thrown just as far off balance as I, or else he wanted—was obliged?—to keep any doubts he may have had to himself. My mind was still mulling over such thoughts when a rather low, self-assured, asthmatic voice came on the tape recorder.

"Monsieur, just so there won't be any misunderstandings—
I will tell you as much of the story as discretion will allow. Inspector Pingaud has vouched for you; still, there are certain
matters that are better left undiscussed. The dossier you brought
with you to Paris is something I've known about for a long
time, longer than you, and I'll give you my honest opinion:
this case doesn't warrant an investigation. Don't take me wrong.
It's just that I have no professional interest in anything that
doesn't come under the penal code. The world's full of mind-
baffling things—flying saucers, exorcisms, guys on TV who can
bend forks from a distance—but none of that means anything
to me as a policeman. Oh, when I read about such things in
France-Soir, I can scratch my head and say, 'Well, I'll be
damned!' I may be wrong in saying the Italian affair doesn't
call for an investigation; then again, I've put in a good thirty
years on the force. You may disagree with me; that's your privilege. Inspector Pingaud had asked me to brief you on a case
I handled a couple of years ago. When I'm finished you'll see
why it was never publicized. At the risk of being rude, I must
warn you that if you ever try to publish any of this material I
shall categorically deny everything. You'll see why. It's a question of *raison d'état,* and I am, after all, a member of the
French police force. Please don't take it personally; it's a matter of professional loyalty. What I'm telling you is standard
procedure.

"The case has now been shelved, though at one time the
police, the Sûreté, and even French counterintelligence were
all in on it. Well, to start with, the subject's name was Dieudonné Proque. Proque is not really a French name; originally
it was Procke. He was a German Jew who, as a young boy,
emigrated to France with his parents during the Hitler regime,
in 1937. His parents belonged to the middle class, thought of
themselves—till the time of the Nazis, that is—as German
patriots, and had distant relatives in Strasbourg whose ancestors
had settled in France in the eighteenth century. I'm going so
far back in time because this was one of those cases calling for

a thorough background investigation. The tougher the case, the more widely the net has to be thrown.

"His father left him nothing when he died, and Proque later became an optician. He spent the occupation years in Marseilles, in the unoccupied zone, where he stayed with relatives. Except for the war years, he lived the whole time in Paris, in my *arrondissement,* where he ran a little optical shop out of his apartment on Rue Amélie. Since he didn't have the resources to compete with the more established firms, business was bad, and he barely made ends meet. He made very little from sales, mostly from repairs—replacing lenses, fixing broken toys, that sort of thing. An optician for the poor. He lived with his mother, a woman going on ninety. A bachelor, he was sixty-one at the time in question. His record was clean: not one court conviction, though we knew the photo lab he'd fixed up at the back of the shop was far from being the innocent little hobby he said it was. There are people who specialize in risqué pictures—not necessarily pornography—but who are unable or unwilling to do their own developing, in which case they need someone else to handle it, someone reliable who won't make extra prints for himself. Within limits, there's not even anything illegal about it. Then there are those who lure people into tricky situations and take pictures for blackmail. We keep most of the blackmailers on file, and it's not advisable for them to have their own darkroom or camera equipment or to hire a photographer who's already had a conviction. Proque was running that kind of racket, but only as a sideline. We knew that he was developing pictures and that he usually did it when he was hard pressed financially. But that was still no reason to move in on him. And frankly, these aren't the only things that get by the police nowadays. Not enough full-time staff, not enough funds, and not enough manpower. Besides, we knew Proque wasn't making a bundle on the deal. He didn't have the nerve to use extortion against any of his clients. He was the cautious type, a coward by nature, completely dominated by his mother. Every July they'd make the same trip to Normandy; they lived always in the same cluttered apartment above the shop, in the same building, with the same neighbors they'd known since before the war. A brief physical description of the man, since that's important for you: short, thin, prematurely stooped, with a tic in his left eye and a constantly drooping eyelid. To those who didn't know him, and especially in the afternoon hours, he gave the impression of being hard of hearing and a bit of a crank. But he was completely in his right mind, except for periodic drowsy spells—usually in the afternoon—caused by low blood pressure. That's why he always kept a Thermos of coffee on his workbench, to help keep him awake on the job. As the years went by, these spells grew worse, to the point where he was constantly yawning and on the verge of fainting or collapsing. Finally his mother made him go to see a doctor. He saw two doctors, both of whom prescribed harmless stimulants, which actually helped for a while.

"What I'm telling you isn't a secret; every tenant in the building knew about it. People even knew about his shady business deals in the darkroom. The guy was so easy to see through. And in the end these pictures were nothing compared to your bread-and-butter sort of stuff. The fact is, I'm in Homicide; morals offenses are not my department. Anyway, what happened later had nothing to do with morals offenses. What else should I tell you to complete the picture? He was a collector of old postcards, used to grumble a lot about having hypersensitive skin—too much exposure to the sun made him break out all over, though he didn't seem like the sort of man who'd go out of his way to get a suntan. But that fall his complexion started to change, became sort of coppery, the way it does when it's been exposed to a sun lamp, and some of his regular customers, friends of his, started saying, 'Tch, tch, Monsieur Proque, don't tell me you've been going to a sunroom?!' And, blushing like a little girl, he'd explain that he had a bad case of boils—in the most sensitive spot, he said—so bad that his doctor had prescribed radiation plus vitamins and a special skin ointment. Apparently the treatment worked.

"That October was especially cold and rainy. Fall was also the time of year the optician was most susceptible to attacks of dizziness and fainting spells, so again he went to see the doctor, and again the doctor prescribed some pep pills. Around the end of the month, while he and his mother were eating dinner one night, he became very excited and began telling her about how he stood to make a killing on a big order for developing and enlarging lots of prints, in color and in large format. He figured on netting sixteen hundred francs on the deal, a small fortune for a man like Proque. At seven that evening he lowered the shutter and, after telling his mother he wouldn't be back till late, shut himself up in his darkroom. Around one in the morning his mother was awakened by a noise coming from her son's room. She found him sitting on the floor and crying 'worse than any man has ever cried before,' to quote the transcript. In a sobbing voice he kept screaming that he'd wasted his whole life and that suicide was the only way out, started ripping up his favorite postcards, knocking over the furniture . . . and there was nothing his mother could do to stop him. Though normally obedient, he completely ignored her. It was like some cheap melodrama. She kept trailing him around the room and yanking at his clothes; he kept looking for some rope, ripped off the curtain cord but was so weak his mother had no trouble getting it away from him; he went for a knife in the kitchen, and as a last resort threatened to go down to the darkroom, where he always kept a supply of lethal chemicals on hand. But then he suddenly went limp, slumped to the floor, and before long was snoring and whining in his sleep. His mother wasn't strong enough to lift him into bed, so she slipped a pillow under his head and let him sleep like that through the night.

"The next morning he was his normal self again, though extremely demoralized. He complained of a bad headache, said he felt as if he'd been drinking the whole night, though in fact all he'd had to drink was a quarter of a bottle of wine at lunch, and a weak table wine at that. After taking a couple of aspirin tablets, he went down to the shop, where he spent a routine day. He had very few customers as an optician, and since he spent most of his time in the back polishing lenses or in the darkroom developing photos, the shop was usually empty. That afternoon he waited on a total of four customers. He kept a record of every order, even the most minor repair job done on the spot. If the customer was a stranger, he'd merely jot down the order. Needless to say, he didn't keep a record of his photographic work.

"The next two days were also uneventful. On the third day he got an advance for the enlargements and prints, though of course he was shrewd enough not to enter this amount in the cash receipts. That night he and his mother ate more extravagantly than usual, at least by their standards: an elegant wine, a special fish dish—oh, I can't remember all the dishes any more, though there was a time when I knew all of them by heart, even what kind of cheeses they ate for dessert. The following day he received another batch of undeveloped film, from the same client. During lunch he was in an excellent mood, telling his mother all about his plans for building a house; then, in the evening, he shut himself up in his darkroom again. Around midnight his mother heard a terrible commotion, went downstairs, stood in the hallway, and knocked on the back door of the darkroom. Through the plywood partition she listened to him ranting and raving, breaking things, turning the place upside down. . . . Panic-stricken, she ran to get her neighbor, an engraver whose workshop was just down the street. The neighbor, an easygoing old widower, used a chisel to pry open the bolt on the partition door.

"It was dark inside, hardly any noise. They found Proque lying on the floor; scattered all around him were the partially developed and still sticky negatives of pornographic photos. They were everywhere, many of them torn and others still glued together. The linoleum floor was covered with chemicals, all the reagent bottles had been smashed to smithereens, the enlarger lay damaged on the floor, there were acid burns on Proque's hands and holes in his clothes, the faucet was running full blast, and he was soaked from head to foot—apparently after trying to revive himself by sticking his head under the faucet. From the looks of it, he'd tried to poison himself, by mistake grabbed some bromide instead of cyanide, and went into a narcotic stupor. He put up no resistance when his neighbor practically carried him back to his apartment. His mother testified that after the neighbor left, Proque tried to go on another rampage but was too worn out physically. The scene that followed was again straight out of some second-rate comedy: he flopped around in his bed, tried to rip up his top sheet to hang himself, stuffed his pillowcase into his mouth, and all the time kept shrieking, crying, swearing. As soon as he tried to get to his feet he collapsed and fell asleep on the floor, as he had the time before.

"He woke up the next day feeling miserable as hell. The sight of all the damage he'd caused only made him feel guiltier and more despondent, so he spent the whole morning picking up the pieces, rinsing things off, trying to salvage what was left of the negatives, and mopping up the mess. When he was finished cleaning up the darkroom, he took his cane—he was having another one of his dizzy spells—and went out to stock up on a new supply of chemicals. That evening he complained about having some sort of mental illness, asked his mother if she knew of any cases of insanity in the family, and refused to believe her when she said she didn't. The very fact that he could accuse her of lying convinced her that he wasn't fully recovered yet, since in the past he wouldn't have dared even to raise his voice to her. Never before had he acted so aggressively, but then she could understand how a person might lose his self-control after two consecutive attacks of hysteria, which would've been enough to make anybody think he was going insane. He promised his mother that if it ever happened again he'd go straight to a psychiatrist. It wasn't like him to make such rash decisions; it had taken him weeks to go see a dermatologist, and then not until his boils were really killing him. Not because he was tightfisted—he had no need to be, since he was medically insured—but because he couldn't put up with the slightest change in his routine.

"Not long after that he had a falling out with his client because several of the pictures turned up missing. We still don't know what transpired between them; it's the only major dark spot in the whole affair.

"The following week passed quietly. Proque became more subdued and never brought up the subject of his mental illness again. That Sunday he and his mother went to see a movie. Then on Monday he went completely berserk. It happened like this. Around eleven in the morning he walked out of the shop without bothering to close the door behind him. Nor did he bother to return his friend's greeting—an Italian who ran a little candy store on the corner—when the man called out to him from in front of the shop. The Italian later testified that Proque looked 'somehow funny.' Proque went straight inside the shop, bought some candy, said he'd pay for it on his way back—which wasn't like him at all—because by then he'd be 'rolling in dough,' climbed into a taxi even though it was a good ten years since he'd last taken one, and told the driver to take him to Avenue de l'Opéra. There he made the driver wait and came back fifteen minutes later yelling and waving an envelope full of cash, gave holy hell to some street tramp who tried to make off with the money, climbed back into the taxi, and told the driver this time to take him to Notre Dame. When he reached the island, he paid the fare with a hundred-franc note —the cabby said he saw only hundred-franc notes inside the envelope—and before the cab had even pulled away from the curb, started to climb over the bridge railing. A passer-by grabbed hold of his leg, there was a scuffle, the cabby jumped out of the car, but not even the two of them could handle him. A gendarme showed up, and together they managed to shove him into the taxi, leaving the hundred-franc notes lying on the sidewalk. When Proque wouldn't stop being hysterical, the gendarme handcuffed him, and they headed straight for the hospital. On the way there, Proque pulled a fast one. After the car drove off he collapsed on the seat, went completely limp, then suddenly lunged forward, and before the gendarme could stop him—they were driving in heavy traffic now—grabbed hold of the steering wheel. The cab rammed straight into a Citroën's front door, pinning the driver's arm between the steering wheel and the door. The gendarme managed to get Proque to the hospital in another taxi. At first the hospital didn't treat his case too seriously, since all he did was stand there in a daze, whimper a little, and refuse to answer any questions. Finally he was admitted for observation, but later, when the chief physician was making his rounds, Proque turned up missing. He was found under the bed, wrapped in a blanket pulled out from under his sheet, and huddled up so close to the wall that it was a while before he was even noticed. He was unconscious from loss of blood, having slashed both wrists with a razor blade smuggled from his clothes into his hospital gown. It took three blood transfusions, but they pulled him through, though he later developed complications due to his poor heart condition.

"I was assigned to the case the day after the incident on the Île St-Louis. Though there was nothing to warrant an investigation by the Sûreté, the lawyer representing the owner of the Citroën, figuring this was a good chance to milk the police, came up with a version charging the police official on duty with criminal negligence. Having in his custody a deranged criminal, the lawyer claimed, the policeman was responsible for allowing the taxicab to collide with his client's car, causing bodily and property damage as well as severe psychological shock to his client. Since the police were criminally liable, any compensation for damages would have to come out of government funds.

"Hoping to gain an advantage, the lawyer leaked his version to the press, which had the effect of escalating the whole affair, since now it was the prestige of the Police Judiciaire that was at stake. It was at this point that I was called in to make an investigation.

"The preliminary medical report indicated Proque had suffered an acute psychosis caused by a delayed attack of schizophrenia, but the longer he was kept under observation after his suicide attempt, the less this diagnosis seemed to hold up. In the space of just six days he had become a thoroughly broken and wasted old man, but he was completely sane in all other respects. On the seventh day of his stay in the hospital he made a deposition. He testified that instead of paying him the sixteen hundred francs they had agreed upon, his client had paid him less than one hundred fifty, for failing to deliver all the prints. That Monday, while he was grinding some lenses for a new fitting, he suddenly became so furious he dropped everything and left the shop, 'to get what he had coming to him.' He had no recollection of going into the candy store or of anything that happened on the bridge, only that his client had come up with the balance of the money after Proque went to his apartment and made a stink. Later that night, after making his deposition, Proque suddenly took a turn for the worse. He died early the next morning of heart failure. The doctors were unanimous in ascribing it to a reactive psychosis.

"Though Proque's death was only indirectly related to Monday's attack, the case was becoming more serious. Nothing like having a corpse for a trump card. The day before he died, I had gone to pay Proque's mother a visit. For a woman her age she turned out to be very cooperative and obliging. On my way out to Rue Amélie I picked up a man from Narcotics to examine the darkroom and the photo-lab chemicals. I was tied up for quite a while with Madame Proque, because once she got started on something there was nothing I could do but sit and listen patiently. Near the end of my visit, I thought I heard the shop's doorbell ring through a crack in the window. I found my helper behind the counter going through the work ledger.

" 'Find anything?' I asked.

" 'Nothing to speak of.'

"His voice betrayed uncertainty.

" 'Did someone come in?'

" 'Yes. How did you know?'

"He then told me what had happened. When the bell rang, he had been standing on a chair searching an electrical cable box, so it was a few seconds before he was able to enter the shop. The customer heard him tinkering around in the back and, thinking it was Proque, called out in a loud voice, 'How are you feeling today, Dieudonné?'

"Just then my assistant came into the shop and spotted a bareheaded, middle-aged man who, the moment he saw him, instinctively made a move for the door. The reason was purely accidental. Normally the Narcotics Squad wore civilian clothes on the job, but that afternoon they were obliged to appear in full uniform for a small decoration ceremony being held in honor of one of their superiors. Since it wasn't scheduled to begin until four, my assistant had decided to wear his uniform to work so he wouldn't have to go home again to change clothes.

"It was obviously the sight of the uniform that had startled the intruder. He said he had come for his glasses and showed the agent his repair tag. The agent explained that the owner of the shop had been incapacitated and that therefore he would have to wait for his glasses. It looked as if there was nothing left to be said, but the stranger refused to leave. Then he asked in a low voice if Proque had suddenly been taken ill. The agent said he had.

" 'Seriously ill?'

" 'Fairly seriously, yes.'

" 'I . . . desperately need those glasses,' the stranger said quite unexpectedly, apparently unable to ask the question uppermost in his mind.

" 'Is he . . . is he still alive?' he blurted out suddenly.

"By now my assistant was getting suspicious. Without giving a reply, he placed his hand on the counter top's hinged lid with the idea of checking the man's identification, but just then the man spun around and left the shop. By the time the agent lifted the counter top and ran outside, the stranger was gone. It was the start of the four o'clock rush hour, a light drizzle was falling, and the sidewalks were packed.

"I was upset that he'd let him get away, but I postponed giving him a reprimand. Besides, we now had the optician's work ledger. I asked the agent whether he could recall the number on the man's repair tag, but it had escaped his notice. The ledger included a number of recent entries, but only the customers' initials were given, which didn't look too promising. Our only other lead was the missing stranger, who knew Proque well enough to call him by his first name. I jotted down the most recent entries, though I wasn't very optimistic. Was the repair tag a pretext or cover? I wondered. But any drugs that well hidden would have meant it was the work of professionals. I didn't know what to make of Proque any more. But even if I'd misjudged the man and his shop *was* being used as a drop, it seemed pretty absurd to think Proque would have helped himself to a dose, much less taken an overdose. The stuff could have been counterfeit, which was often the case, but it was unusual for dealers and middlemen to use narcotics themselves: they're too well acquainted with the aftereffects to be tempted. I was nearly at the end of my wits when my assistant suddenly recalled that, even though it had been raining, the stranger had been without an umbrella or a hat, and that his mohair coat was almost completely dry. We knew he couldn't have come by car, because the street had been blocked off for repairs, so chances were that he lived somewhere in the neighborhood. It took us five days to track him down. How did we find him? Very simple. Based on the agent's description a composite sketch was made of the missing man and circulated among all the concierges on Rue Amélie. The man identified was a prominent scientist, a doctor of chemistry by the name of Dunant. Jérôme Dunant. While going through the ledger I'd noticed something unusual: the initials J. D. were listed on each of the three days preceding Proque's attacks. The doctor lived a few doors down the street, so early one afternoon I went to call on him. When he met me at the door, I recognized him at once from the sketch.

" 'Oh, yes,' he said. 'Come right in.'

" 'It looks as if you were expecting me,' I said as I followed him inside.

" 'I was. Is Proque still alive?'

" 'I beg your pardon, but it was *I* who wanted to ask *you* a few questions, not vice versa. What makes you think Proque might not be alive?'

" 'Now it's my turn not to answer. You see, inspector, it's absolutely essential there be no publicity about this. It *must* be kept out of the press. Otherwise the consequences could be disastrous.'

" 'Disastrous for whom? For yourself?'

" 'For France.'

"I ignored this last comment but couldn't get any more out of him.

" 'I'm sorry,' he said, 'but any statement I make will have to be to the head of the Sûreté, and then not before I have special clearance from my superiors.'

"He volunteered no other information, afraid I might be one of those policemen who like to pass on sensational news stories to the media. That I found out only afterward. He gave us quite a hard time, but in the end he got his way. My superior got in touch with his superior, and two ministries had to approve before he was allowed to testify.

"It's a well-known fact that every nation loves peace and makes plans for war. France is no exception. Chemical warfare is always treated with moral indignation, but still the research goes on. It just so happened that Dr. Dunant was working on a project aimed at developing chemical compounds known as psychotropic depressants, which in pill or gas form would be capable of paralyzing the enemy's will and morale. Under the seal of secrecy we were told that for over four years Dr. Dunant had been trying to synthesize such a depressant. By working with a certain chemical compound, he had obtained a number of derivatives, one of which proved to be capable of producing the desired effect on the brain but only when administered in massive doses. Only when taken by the spoonful did it produce the symptomatic effects of hyperexcitability and aggression, followed by depression, and culminating in an acute suicidal mania. Finding the right compound is very often a matter of luck, arrived at by substituting various chemical groups in the original compound and then analyzing the derivatives for their pharmacological properties. Sometimes it can take years of research to find the right combination; other times one can achieve instantaneous results, the latter being of course the exception, rather than the rule.

"Since he was extremely nearsighted, Dr. Dunant was forced to wear his glasses at all times. For the past several years he had been a steady customer of Proque's. Since he was severely handicapped without his glasses, he made it a point always to keep three pairs on hand. He would wear one pair, carry the second pair around with him as a spare, and keep the third pair at home. He'd begun taking these precautions after breaking a pair of glasses in the lab and having to interrupt his work as a result. And just before his last visit to the shop—three weeks before, to be exact—he had had another accident. Dunant worked in a maximum-security laboratory. Before entering the lab he would have to change into a new set of clothes, including special shoes and underwear, and deposit all his personal items in a changing room separated from the work area by a pressure chamber. While he worked he was required to wear a transparent plastic hood equipped with its own air supply system. At no time was his body or glasses allowed to come into contact with any of the chemical substances under investigation. To avoid any further possible inconvenience, he had got into the habit of putting his extra pair of glasses on one of the reagent shelves before going to work. One day, as he was reaching for a reagent, he accidentally knocked them to the floor, shattering one lens and damaging the frame by stepping on it with his foot. He immediately took them to Proque for repair, but two days later, when he went to pick them up, he hardly recognized the optician, who had the tired and haggard look of someone who's just recovered from a serious illness. Proque told him he suspected having been poisoned, because the night before he'd been overcome by a strange attack that for some reason made him feel like crying even now.

"Dunant quickly forgot about Proque and his troubles, but he was far from satisfied with the repair job: not only did one of the stems pinch, but also one of the newly fitted lenses came loose from its plastic frame and finally popped out and broke on the laboratory's tiled floor. Dunant brought the glasses back a second time, but when he stopped by for them the following day Proque seemed to have aged overnight. Casually he began inquiring about the details of this latest 'attack.' Proque's description sounded like an acute depression caused by a chemically induced psychosis, very similar, in fact, to the symptoms produced by the compound X he had been working on. But since it would have taken a hefty dose of at least ten grams in pure form to provoke such a violent reaction, he failed to see what connection this could have with the glasses. Twice he had brought for repair the pair that usually lay on the reagent shelf located above the Bunsen burner. Then he began wondering whether the chemical fumes might have traveled through the air and settled on the glasses in microscopic amounts. He decided to run a test on them. By subjecting the glasses to a chemical analysis, he established that traces of the compound were indeed present on the lenses and frame stems, but in amounts measurable in gammas—in other words, in micrograms. The story of how LSD was discovered is a familiar one among chemists. Like everyone else at the time, the chemist experimenting with it was completely unaware of its hallucinogenic effects. But after returning home from work one night, he started experiencing all the symptoms of a 'trip'—visions, psychic manifestations, and the like—though before leaving the lab he had washed his hands as thoroughly as he always did.

But the infinitesimal amount lodged under his fingernails had been enough to induce the symptoms while he was making dinner.

"Dunant began thinking how an optician goes about installing a new set of lenses and adjusting the stems. He recalled that the synthetically made stems are passed quickly back and forth over a gas flame. Could the heat have altered the chemical composition of the compound, in a way that it made its effect a million times more potent? Taking samples of the compound, Dunant tried heating them by every means possible—with burners, spirit lamps, candle flame—but with no results. At that point he decided to perform the *experimentum crucis*. He deliberately bent one of the stems and bathed it with a thin enough solution of compound X so that a residue amounting to one-millionth of a gram remained on the frame after the solvent had evaporated. He then brought the glasses back to the optician for the third time. This was the pair he had come to pick up when he saw the agent behind the counter.

"There you have the whole story, monsieur, a story without a solution or an end. Dr. Dunant theorized that the chemical alteration was caused by something in the optician's workshop and that the resulting catalytic reaction made the chemical's effect a million times more powerful. But since nothing was found to corroborate his theory, we decided to drop the case: if you have to chase after atoms instead of people, then it's time to call off the investigation. No crime was committed, since the amount smeared by Dr. Dunant on the glasses was barely enough to kill a fly, much less the optician. I later heard that Dunant—or someone acting on his behalf—acquired the contents of the darkroom from Madame Proque and tested all the reagents for their effect on compound X, but without any results.

"Madame Proque died before Christmas that same year. In the department it was rumored that after her death Dunant spent the whole winter in the abandoned shop and during that time took samples of everything—the plywood partition, the grinding stone, the varnish on the wall, the dust on the floor—but found nothing. It was Inspector Pingaud who insisted I tell you the whole story. I suspect your Naples case falls into the same category. Now that the world has reached a state of scientific perfection, such things are bound to happen. That's all I have to say."

Because of the traffic, it took us nearly an hour to drive back to Garges. Neither of us said very much along the way. The story of Proque's gradual insanity was as familiar to me as the back of my own hand. All that was missing was the hallucination phase, but, then, who knows what sort of visions the poor bastard might have had. Funny, all along I'd been treating the other victims like the pieces of a puzzle, but Proque was different. I felt sorry for him. Thanks to Dunant. Oh, I could understand that mice weren't enough. Mice couldn't be driven to suicide. For that he needed a human being. He wasn't taking any risks, either: the moment he saw a cop at the door, he could always use France as an alibi. Even that I could understand. But what made me so furious was that "How are you feeling today, Dieudonné?" of his. If that Japanese assassin in Rome was a criminal, then what was Dunant? I bet Dunant wasn't even his real name. Why had the inspector let me listen to the story? I wondered. Not out of sympathy, that's for sure. And what was the *real* story behind all this? The ending could have been faked, too. If that was the case, then the whole thing could have been staged as a harmless pretext for relaying information to the Pentagon about a new type of chemical weapon.

The more I thought about it, the more plausible this seemed. They'd shown their hand so well that if worst came to worst, they could always deny everything. Even *they* had said they came away empty-handed, and how the hell was I to tell whether they were telling the truth. If I'd been your ordinary private detective, you can be sure they wouldn't have bothered with such a show; but an astronaut, even a second-string one, has ties with NASA, and NASA has ties with the Pentagon. If the whole thing was planned by the higher-ups, then Pingaud was merely carrying out orders, and Barth's confusion wasn't to be taken at face value, either. Barth was in a far trickier situation than I. He, too, must have detected an element of big-league politics in this unexpected "generosity" of theirs, but he didn't feel it was worth telling me about because it must have taken him by surprise. I was sure he hadn't been tipped off in advance; I knew enough about the rules of the game to know that. They couldn't very well take him aside and say, "OK, all we have to do is show that Yank one of our high cards and he's bound to pass it on." That's just not the way it's done. And it would have looked funny as hell if they'd clued me in and not Barth, especially when they knew he'd already promised me the use of his team. No, they could afford neither to leave him out nor to bring him in, so they did the next most sensible thing: they let him hear exactly what I heard and then left him to worry about the implications on his own. I would have bet he was sorry he ever offered me his help. Then I started meditating on what all this meant in terms of the investigation. It didn't present a very rosy picture. From the Italian series we'd deduced a number of qualifying factors: the mineral baths, men past the age of fifty, sturdy physique, bachelors, sun, allergy, and here was someone well over sixty, skinny, not allergic to anything, living with his mother, who never took sulfur baths, never got a tan, and hardly ever left the house! In fact, he couldn't have been a more dissimilar type. In a fit of magnanimity I suggested to Barth that each of us digest this latest bit of news on his own, to avoid influencing the other, and compare notes later on that evening. He was all for it.

Around three I went into the garden, where little Pierre was waiting for me. This meeting was our very own secret. He showed me the parts of his rocket. The first stage was a washtub. No one is more sensitive than a child, so I did not mention that a washtub wasn't exactly cut out to be a booster rocket, and I drew for him on the sand the various stages of a Saturn V and IX.

At five I went to keep my appointment with Barth in the library. He took me somewhat by surprise when he led off by saying that since France was doing research on factor X, it was safe to assume that other countries were engaged in similar research. Such work, he said, was always carried out on a parallel basis, in which case even the Italians might have ... Maybe it was time to re-examine the whole affair. The compound wouldn't have had to come from a government lab; it could also have originated in a private company. It might have been developed by a chemist connected with the extremists, or, as seemed more likely, some of it might have been pirated. Perhaps the people in charge of administering it did not know how to exploit it to its maximal effect, and so they decided to conduct some experiments. But, then, why were the victims all foreigners, all in the same age group, all rheumatics, and so on?

He had an answer for that as well.

"Put yourself in the place of the group's leader. You've heard about the chemical's powerful reaction, but you're not exactly sure *what* kind of effect it has. Since you're a man without any moral scruples, you decide to try it out on various people. But which people? You can't very well test it out on your own members. So who? On just anyone? That would mean an Italian, with a family. But since the initial symptoms would be interpreted as a personality change, an Italian would very soon wind up under a doctor's care or as a patient in a clinic. A single man, however, can do just about anything before anyone will take notice, especially in hotels, where every sort of whim is indulged. And the better the hotel, the greater the isolation. At a third-class boardinghouse, the landlady is likely to keep a watchful eye on her tenants' every move, whereas at the Hilton you can walk around on your hands and still not attract any attention. Neither the management nor the employees will bat an eyelash as long as it doesn't involve a criminal offense. Speaking a foreign language is another isolating factor. So far so good?"

"What about the other factors—age, allergy, rheumatism, the sulfur treatments?"

"The greater the difference in behavior before and after the chemical agent has been administered, the more meaningful the test results. A young man is always on the go; one day he's in Naples, the next day he's in Sicily. An older man makes an ideal subject, especially if he's a patient at a health spa, where all his movements—from the doctor's office to the baths, from the sunroom to the hotel—are likely to be according to schedule, in which case the drug's effects will be more noticeable. . . ."

"What about the sex factor?"

"It wasn't a coincidence that all the victims were men. Why? Because they were out to get only men in the first place. This seems crucial to me, because it would seem to point to an underlying political motive. If it's high-ranking politicians you're after, then it's only logical for you to choose men. . . . What do you think?"

"You might have something there . . ." I admitted, suddenly awed by the prospect. "So you think they might have had people planted in the hotels and selected a certain type of guest matching in age those politicians they were planning to assassinate as part of a *coup d'état?* Is that what you had in mind?"

"I'm not one for jumping to conclusions. It's better not to limit the scope of the inquiry. . . . Well now, fifteen or twenty years ago such an idea would have smacked of a gimmicky potboiler or thriller, but today. . . . You see what I mean?"

I saw what he meant, and sighed: I didn't enjoy the prospect of reopening the investigation. I quickly weighed the pros and cons.

"I have to admit I'm speechless. . . . But there are still quite a few things to be explained. Why only people with allergies? And what about the baldness? Or the time of year—the end of May, beginning of June? Have you got an explanation for these as well?"

"No. At least not an immediate one. In my opinion one

should start from the other end, by classifying not the 'experi-mental' victims but the *real* victims, the ones actually intended. That would mean going down the list of Italy's political élite. If it turned out that there were a few with allergy problems. . . ."

"I see! In other words, you're sending me back to Rome. And I'm afraid I'll have to go; this could be the hottest lead so far. . . ."

"There's no need for you to leave right away, is there?"

"Tomorrow or the next day at the latest. These are things that can't be handled over the phone."

We left it at that. The more I thought over Barth's theory in my room, the more ingenious I found it. Not only had he put forward a plausible hypothesis, but he'd also managed to get himself off the hook by referring the matter to Rome and side-stepped the whole issue of France's involvement with compound X. This way it no longer mattered whether Dunant actually succeeded in reconstructing the chemical in the darkroom on Rue Amélie. The more I thought about it, the more positive I became that Barth's version was right on target. Compound X not only existed but also worked. I was sure of it, just as I was sure that such a method for political assassination couldn't help but have a tremendous impact—and not only in Italy—an impact even greater than that of a "classic" *coup d'état*.

I now began to view the case of the eleven with an antipathy bordering on disgust. What was once an inscrutable mystery had now been turned into a struggle for power as crass as it was bloody. Behind all the bizarre appearances was something as trite as political murder.

The next day I headed straight for Rue Amélie. I don't really know why. But around eleven there I was, walking down the sidewalk and browsing in the shopwindows, though even as I was leaving Garges I was still debating whether I shouldn't re-consider and go by way of the Eiffel Tower to bid farewell to Paris. But once I reached the boulevards it was too late for that. I didn't know my way around this part of Paris, so I had trouble finding the street, and it took me a while to find a parking place. I recognized Proque's apartment even before I could make out the number. It looked more or less as I'd imagined it would, an old apartment building with closed shutters and that old-fashioned trim around the gables with which architects of the last century used to lend their buildings a touch of individuality. The optician's shop was defunct, the shutter lowered and padlocked. On my way back I stopped in front of a toy store. It was time to shop around for some souvenirs, because I had no intention of taking part in a new investigation; I'd pass on all the information to Randy and then head back to the States. My mind made up, I went inside to buy something for my sister's boys—as a way of justifying this latest lark of mine. On the shelves our whole civilization was gaudily arrayed in miniature. I looked around for toys I remembered from childhood but found only electronic gadgets, rocket launchers, and miniature supermen shown in judo or karate attack positions. You dope, I told myself, who are the toys for, anyway?

I decided on a couple of plumed parade helmets—the kind worn by the French Guard—and a Marianne puppet, because these were toys you couldn't get in Detroit. As I was heading back to the car with my packages, I spotted a candy store with white curtains on the corner. In the display window was a bronze-colored Vesuvius covered with roasted almonds; I was reminded of the almond peddler I used to pass on my way from the hotel to the beach. I wasn't sure the boys would like the bitter-tasting almonds, but I went in and bought a couple of bags anyway. How strange, I thought, that of all places Naples should be saying good-bye to me here. Grudgingly I made my way back to the car, as if I still hadn't given up—given *what* up? I didn't know; maybe it was the purity that all along I'd unconsciously attached to the mystery. I threw the packages down on the back seat and, standing there with one hand on the open car door, said good-bye to Rue Amélie. Was there any more reason to doubt Leclerc's words or Barth's hypothesis? All my wildest, most private conjectures vanished. But had

I ever really believed I would make some startling discovery, that I would splice together all the details in a way no one had ever done before and by some stroke of genius arrive at the hitherto undisclosed truth? Here and there vestiges of the old Paris were still to be seen, but they were destined to be obliterated, wiped out by that army of Molochs at Défense. I had lost all desire to visit the Eiffel Tower. By now Dr. Dunant would already be at work in his porcelain and nickel-plated labs. I had visions of him wrapped in his synthetic turban, eyes aglitter over the distilling apparatus, the coiled air hose trailing behind his plastic cocoon. I was more than familiar with that world: in Houston I had seen the most exquisite labs, the sterile church naves of rocket domes.

I no longer felt like taking in the scenery as I used to do before takeoff, moments before everything collapsed below me. I had such a bad feeling that I jumped behind the wheel, but before I had a chance to start the car my nose began tickling. Angrily I held my breath for a moment; then the sneezing started. Thunder rumbled across the rooftops, the sky was turning darker, and a cloudburst hung overhead. I blew my nose and went on sneezing, but now I was laughing at myself. The blooming season was catching up with me in Paris, and the worst time was always just before a storm. I reached into the glove compartment, but the Plimasine got stuck in my throat and fell apart into bitter-tasting pieces. For lack of anything better, I tore open the bag of almonds and munched on them all the way back to Garges.

I like driving in the rain, so I took my time. On the highway the steam given off by the rain was turned a dirty shade of silver by the headlights. It was a fierce but short storm, so that by the time I climbed out of the car in front of the house, the rain had stopped. I wasn't meant to leave town that day, I guess, because on my way down to the dining room I slipped on the stairs—they'd just been freshly polished by the Spanish maid—leaving me doubled up and with an aching tail bone. At the dinner table I tried to play it down and chatted with the old lady, who was sure I'd injured a disc and said that there was no better cure for that than flowers of sulfur, the universal remedy for every sort of rheumatic ailment, and that all I had to do was to sprinkle it under my shirt. I thanked her for the sulfur powder and, realizing it was impossible for me to fly to Rome in this condition, willingly accepted Barth's offer to take me to a famous Parisian chiropractor.

Accompanied by expressions of sympathy, I dragged myself upstairs and crawled into bed like a cripple. I managed to fall asleep after finding the least painful position, but later woke up sneezing, having inhaled some sort of acrid powder coming from underneath my pillow. I jumped out of bed and let out a howl: I had forgotten about my back. At first I thought the Spanish maid, in an excess of zeal, had sprinkled the sheets with an insecticide, but it turned out to be that infallible remedy for rheumatism that good old Pierre had secretly administered while I was at the dinner table. I shook the yellow dust out of the sheet, pulled the cover over my head, and dozed off to the steady patter of raindrops pounding on the roof.

At breakfast time, I descended the stairs as if lowering myself down an icy rope ladder on a whaler caught in an arctic storm: a belated precaution. The chiropractor recommended by Barth turned out to be an American black; after taking X-rays and hanging the films on a viewer above the examining table, he went to work on me with hands like paddles. I experienced a sharp but fleeting pain, crawled down from the table under my own power, and discovered that I really did feel a lot better. I had to lie on my back in the office for another half hour, but after that I headed for the nearest Air France office and booked an evening flight. I tried to reach Randy by phone, but he wasn't in his hotel, so I left a message for him.

Back at Barth's house it occurred to me that I had nothing for Pierre, so I promised to send him my space helmet from the States, said good-bye to the whole family, then left for Orly. There I went straight to a Fleurop shop, ordered some flowers for Mrs. Barth, and settled down in a waiting room filled with American newspapers. I sat and sat, but still there was no boarding announcement. I now looked on the case as if it were a thing of the past. Still undecided about the future, I tried—but without success—to glamorize this indecision of mine. Meanwhile our departure time passed, and a steady but indistinct stream of apologies came over the loudspeaker. Then a stewardess stepped out of an office and regretfully announced that Rome was no longer taking any incoming flights.

There was a lot of running around and a flurry of phone calls until it was finally confirmed that in façt Rome was accepting only American planes, Alitalia, and BEA, whereas Swissair, SAS, and my Air France were canceling all departures until further notice. It seems a selective strike had been called by ground personnel, though the reason for the strike was lost in the stampede to exchange tickets and reservations for those airlines that had been given landing clearance. Before I could even fight my way through to the ticket counter, all the seats had been snatched up by the more enlightened passengers. The next available flight was on BEA, scheduled to leave the following day at a God-awful time—at 5:40 A.M. I had little choice: I had my ticket rewritten for the BEA flight, loaded my bags onto a cart, and headed for the Hotel Air France, where I'd spent the first night after my arrival from Rome. There I was in for another surprise. The hotel was filled to capacity with passengers stranded in the same way I was. I was now faced with the prospect of spending the night in Paris and getting up at four o'clock in the morning to make my 5:40 flight. There was no point in going back to Garges, either, since it was situated to the north of Paris and Orly to the south. I shoved my way through the crowd of disappointed passengers, reached the exit, and debated my next move. I could always postpone my departure a day, but that was the last thing I felt like doing: there's nothing worse than a long delay.

I was still deliberating what to do when a man carrying a stack of magazines stepped out of a kiosk and began arranging them on the newsstand. My attention was caught by the latest edition of *Paris-Match*. Staring at me from the black front cover was a man shown suspended in midair like a gymnast executing a side vault. He was wearing suspenders and holding against his chest a child with streaming hair whose head was tilted back in the manner of a trapeze artist. Not believing my own eyes, I walked up to the newsstand. It was a picture taken of Annabella and me. I bought a copy of the magazine, which automatically flipped open to the page featuring the exclusive cover story. Stretched across the entire page in bold letters above a picture of the demolished and body-strewn escalator was the following headline: WE'D RATHER DIE FACING FORWARD. I skimmed through the report. They'd tracked down Annabella, and on the next page was a picture of her with her family—but nowhere was my name mentioned. The photos came from the video tape used by the airport to photograph all those passing through the Labyrinth. I hadn't counted on the publicity. I was relying on their promises of strict confidentiality. I ran through the text again; it was accompanied by a sketch of the escalator and the detonation tank, with arrows indicating the path of my escape, and an enlarged detail from the cover photo showing a checkered sleeve situated between my pant legs and the landing. The caption underneath described it as the arm of the assassin blown off by the explosion. What I'd have given to buttonhole the author of that article! What was stopping him from mentioning me by name? Oh, I figured in it, all right—as "the astronaut." But Annabella's name was there, that "lovely teen-aged girl" who was still waiting for a letter from her rescuer. Though it wasn't made explicit, there were sly insinuations that the airport disaster had given rise to a love affair. A cold fury took hold of me; I wheeled around, elbowed my way through the crowd in the lobby, and barged into the manager's office, where people were all talking at the same time. Cashing in on my recent heroism, I threw the *Paris-Match* down on the manager's desk and started outshouting everyone. I still blush with shame whenever I think back on that scene, but I got my way. The manager, unaccustomed to dealing with heroic astronauts, finally broke down and gave me his last vacancy, swearing up and down that it really was his last when the other passengers suddenly pounced on him like a pack of hounds let off their leashes.

I started to go for my bags but was told the room wouldn't be ready till eleven o'clock; it was still only eight. I left my luggage at the reception desk and found myself in command of three hours' leisure. I regretted having made a spectacle of myself, and since there could have been serious repercussions if a member of the press had happened to be present, I decided to keep a safe distance from the hotel till eleven. I wasn't in the mood for going to a movie or eating out, so on a whim I decided to do something I'd once thought of doing in Quebec when my plane was grounded by a blizzard. I headed for the other end of the terminal, strolled into a barbershop, and ordered the works. The barber was a Gascon, so much of what he said was lost on me, but, sticking to my decision, I agreed to all the frills in order not to risk being hustled out of the chair. After a fairly routine haircut and shampoo, he shifted into high gear. Tuning in some rock-and-roll music on a transistor standing between the mirrors, he turned up the volume, rolled up his sleeves, and, tapping his foot to the music, started to go to town. He patted my face, pulled my cheeks, tweaked my chin, slapped a steaming compress over my eyes and nose, now and then made a small air hole in the burning-hot towel to keep me from suffocating, and asked me a question that I didn't catch because my ears were still plugged with the cotton wads he'd put there before cutting my hair. My "*ça va, bien*" sent him scurrying to his cabinet for more bottles and lotions. Altogether I spent about an hour in the barber's chair. Toward the end he combed and evened out my eyebrows, stepped back, and examined me with a critical frown; then he changed my apron, took out of a separate compartment a small, gold-covered bottle that he held up for my inspection as if it were some classy wine, smeared some green jelly on his fingers, and began rubbing it into my scalp. All this was accompanied by a steady stream of uninterrupted patter, the gist of which was that my worrying days were over now: I would never grow bald. After brushing my hair with a series of brisk strokes, he took away all the hand towels and compresses, pulled the cotton out of my ears, blew into each ear in a way that was both gentle and intimate, showered me with powder, snapped his towel in front of my face, then stepped back and made a dignified bow. He was pleased with himself. With tightened scalp and cheeks aglow, I got up from the chair in a daze, tipped him ten francs, and walked out of the shop.

With some time to go before my room would be ready, I started heading for the observation deck to take in the airport at night but somehow got lost. They were doing some repair work inside the terminal; one section of the escalator was roped off, and mechanics were making a lot of racket in the shafts below. Somehow I drifted into a crowd of people racing toward the departure area. Soldiers in foreign uniforms, nuns in starched bonnets, long-legged blacks who looked to be members of a men's basketball team . . . Bringing up the rear was a stewardess pushing a wheelchair in which a gray-haired man in dark glasses sat holding a furry bundle in his lap; suddenly the bundle jumped down and started crawling toward me on all fours. A monkey dressed in a green jacket and a tiny skullcap stared up at me with darting black eyes, then pirouetted around and started hopping after the moving wheelchair. The rock-and-roll music coming from the barbershop was so infectious I could hear it reverberating in peoples' footsteps and voices. Standing alongside the wall under some neon lights was a TV hockey game; I dropped in a coin and batted the luminous dot around till my eyes began to hurt, then got up and left before my turn was up. Passengers were still streaming toward departures. Among them was a peacock; it stood calmly with its tail lowered, narrowly missing getting hit, and its head tilted to one side as if it were trying to decide whose leg to peck first. Somebody must have lost a peacock, I thought. Unable to fight the crowd, I circled around, but by the time I reached the spot where the peacock had been it was gone.

I thought again of the observation deck but took the wrong corridor by mistake and wound up downstairs in a maze of jewelers, fur shops, foreign-exchange offices, and myriad other little shops. Pausing idly in front of the shop windows, I had the sensation of standing on top of a frozen lake and looking down into its deepest, blackest part. It was much as if the terminal had its own mute and murky negative counterpart underneath. To be more exact, I was conscious of the abyss without actually seeing or feeling anything. I took the escalator upstairs but wound up in another wing, in a hall full of golf carts, dune buggies, and beach cars that stood in narrow rows waiting to be loaded. Squeezing my way through the aisles, I had fun with the fluorescent sheen given off by their luminous bodies, an effect I attributed to the lighting and to the new enamel finish. I paused in front of one buggy that was glazed a metallic gold and caught a glimpse of my own reflection—a quivering mass of yellow with a face that kept stretching vertically and then horizontally; when I held my head in a certain position, my eyes became dark holes secreting black metal beetles; when I leaned forward, another, darker, and more imposing reflection would appear behind my own. I glanced around—no one—but the figure mirrored in gold refused to go away. An uncanny optical illusion. The hall was sealed off by a sliding door at the other end, so I went back the way I came, my every movement and gesture mockingly reflected by my surroundings as in a hall of mirrors. I was somehow disturbed by this proliferation of images. Then I realized it was because the reflections were mimicking me but with a slight delay in time, even though that would have been impossible. To drown out the rock-and-roll tune banging away in my head, I started whistling "John Brown's Body."

I wasn't having any luck finding the observation deck, so I took a side exit and went outside. Despite the proximity of the streetlights, the night was so black and palpably thick you could have squeezed it with your hands: a real African night. It occurred to me that I might have been coming down with night blindness, that something might have been wrong with my rhodopsin, but gradually my vision improved. Must have been that excursion through the gold-plated gallery, I thought—my old eyes can't adjust to the change of light the way they used to.

A huge building was under construction in a lighted area beyond the parking lots. Bulldozers crawled in and out of the columns of light, pushing their loads of shimmering gold sand. A flat cloud of fiery quicksilver hung over this nocturnal Sahara like the Milky Way, while time and again flashes of lightning stitched the backdrop in slow motion—the headlights of cars turning off the highway for the airport. There was something strangely magical in this otherwise ordinary spectacle. It was then that my return trip through the terminal began to take on an aura of anticipation—not of the hotel room, though I hadn't forgotten about it, but of something more important. The fateful moment was approaching. It had the mark of absolute certainty, but, like a man struggling with a name on the tip of his tongue, I couldn't put my finger on it, on what it was I was expecting.

At the main entrance I started mingling with the crowd, or, rather, I was swept up and flung inside. I decided it was time to get a bite to eat at a snack bar. My hot dog tasted as bland as paper; I tossed the half-eaten hot dog and its plastic plate into the trash can and went into a café with a peacock stationed over the entrance in full array. It was much too big to have been stuffed. A week ago Annabella and I had sat under the very same peacock while waiting for her father. There were others in the café. I sat down with my coffee at a corner table, my back to the wall: while standing at the counter I had been conscious of someone staring at me from the rear. No one was looking my way now—to the point where it was blatantly obvious. The distant whine of the jet engines now seemed to come from another, more important world. I sat there using my spoon to break up the sugar lumps at the bottom of my cup.

A magazine with a black cover and a red band running across the top lay on the table next to me—a copy of *Paris-Match,* I guessed—but a woman sitting with her dark-haired Romeo had managed to cover the title with her purse. On purpose, probably. Someone had spotted me, but who? An autograph hound? Some passing reporter? I dropped a copper ashtray on the floor, pretending it was an accident. Despite the noise, no one turned around. Suspicions confirmed. Not wanting to be harassed, I gulped down the rest of my coffee and walked out. I was in a bad way: legs like a couple of hollow pipes, an aching tail bone that served as a painful reminder of the recent past. . . .

Suddenly I was fed up with all the stalling around, so I made my way past the glittering shopwindows and aimed for the escalator marked AIR FRANCE in big sky-blue letters. It was a short-cut to the hotel. I held on tightly to the railing: the combed treads on the steps were slippery, and I wasn't about to take any chances. Halfway between levels I noticed that standing in front of me was a woman with a dog in her arms. I winced: her hair was the exact same shade of blond. Slowly I glanced back over my shoulder, though I had a pretty good hunch who would be standing behind me. A flat face, a complexion made livid by the fluorescent lighting, sunglasses. I shoved my way past the blonde and worked my way up the escalator, but I couldn't just walk off without satisfying my curiosity. So I stood by the railing and inspected the passengers as the escalator dropped them off one by one on the landing. The blonde gave me the once-over as she strolled by. She was carrying a folded shawl with a knotted fringe, the same fringe I'd taken for a dog's tail. The guy in back of me turned out to be fat and pasty-looking. Not a trace of Mongol blood. *Esprit de l'escalier,* I thought—but a week later?! Man, are you ever in bad shape—what you need is a good night's sleep!

Along the way I picked up a bottle of Schweppes, slipped it into my coat pocket, and glanced at the clock above the reception desk with a sigh of relief: my room would be ready. My bellboy went ahead of me with my bags, set the smaller one down on top of the larger one in the hallway, pocketed a ten-franc tip, and was on his way. The hotel breathed a quiet sort of intimacy that made the whining roar of a landing airplane seem incongruous. Good thing I'd remembered to pick up a Schweppes. I was thirsty now, but, not having a bottle opener, I peeked into the corridor to see if there was a refrigerator where I might be able to lay my hands on one. The warm colors of the hallway carpet and walls caught my eye, filling me with respect and admiration for French interior decorators. I found a refrigerator, opened the bottle of Schweppes, and was already heading back to my room when who should come around the corner but Annabella. In a dark dress she looked taller than I'd remembered her, but she had the same white ribbon in her hair; and when she came toward me, swinging her shoulder bag at her side, it was with the same serious look in her dark eyes. I recognized the purse, too, though the last time I'd seen it, it had been ripped open at the seams. I'd left the door open on my way out, and she slipped into the doorway.

"Annabella, what're you doing here?" I wanted to say, being as shocked as I was glad to see her, but all I could muster was a faint "Aa—" before she went inside the room, with such an inviting toss of the head and with such an unequivocal glance of the eyes that I stopped dead in my tracks. She left the inner door open, and in my momentary panic I thought maybe she wanted to confide in me, but before I was even in the room I distinctly heard both her shoes fall to the floor and the bed squeak. With these sounds still fresh in my ears, feeling morally indignant, I went in and gasped: the room was empty.

"Annabella!" I yelled. The bed was untouched. "Annabella!" Silence. In the bathroom, maybe? I opened the door, but it was dark inside; I waited in the doorway till the light blinked on. Bathtub, bidet, towel rack, washbasin, my own reflection in the mirror . . . I went back into the room, not daring to call out any more. Though it was unlikely she would have had time to hide in the wardrobe cabinet, I opened it anyway. Empty. My knees began to buckle, so I slumped into an armchair. Even now I could describe exactly the way she walked, the kind of clothes she wore. . . . Then I realized why she'd seemed taller: she was wearing high heels instead of sandals. I could still see that expression in her eyes as she passed through the doorway, the way her hair spilled over her shoulder when she motioned with her head. I could still hear her naughtily kicking off her shoes and the sound made by the creaking bedsprings, and I remembered my jabbing, stinging sensation at hearing those sounds. . . . Was it all just a fantasy? A hallucination?

I touched my knees, my chest, and my face, as if this were the sequence in which I had to examine them, ran my hands over the chair's rough upholstery, walked across the room and banged my fist against the wardrobe's half-open door; everything felt solid, stationary, immutable, well defined, and yet somehow ambiguous. I paused in front of the television set and saw a reduced reflection of the bed and a pair of girls' shoes carelessly flung down on the carpet. I spun around in horror.

There was nothing on the floor, nothing anywhere. Next to the television set was a telephone. I picked up the receiver, heard the dial tone, but stopped short of dialing. What was I to tell Barth—that I was in a hotel fantasizing about some girl and was afraid to be left alone? I hung up the receiver, took my toilet kit out of my suitcase, went into the bathroom; as I leaned over the basin, I suddenly froze. Everything I was doing had its immediate and familiar precedent. Like Proque I splashed my face with cold water. Like Osborn I rubbed my temples with cologne. Then I went back into the room, not knowing what to do next. Nothing happened to me. The most sensible thing would have been to climb into bed and go to sleep. On the other hand, I was afraid of undressing, as if my clothes were somehow a protection. Moving quietly in order not to rouse the evil spirit, I took off my pants, shoes, and shirt, and after switching off the overhead light, pressed my head against the pillow. Now the threat seemed to come from outside—from the hazy ambiguity of the objects standing in the penumbra of the night light. I switched off the lamp. A feeling of inertia came over me; I forced myself to take long and even breaths. There was a knock at the door; I didn't move a muscle. There was another knock, and someone—a man—opened the door and stepped into the passageway. The figure, silhouetted against the corridor's brightness, started advancing toward my bed.

"Monsieur . . ."

I didn't make a sound. Now so close that he stood over me, he laid something down on the table and quietly withdrew. The lock on the door clicked; I was alone again. I dragged myself out of bed—more beat than dazed—and switched on the wall light. Lying on the table was a telegram. With a pounding heart and wobbly legs I picked it up. It was addressed to me, care of the Hotel Air France. I glanced down at the sender's name, and my blood ran cold. I pressed my eyelids together, opened the telegram, and again read the name of the man who had been buried long enough to be a rotting corpse.

WAITING ROME HILTON RM 303

ADAMS

I must have read and reread the message ten times, examining the telegram up close and from every angle. It had left Rome at 10:40, thus well over an hour ago. It was probably just a slip of the pen. Randy might have moved into the Hilton —he had settled for the little hotel near the Spanish Steps for lack of anything better—and this was his way of letting me know. Or he might have received my message, given up waiting for me, then heard about the flight cancellations and decided to wire me. But why the switch in names? And of all names, why that one? I sat down by the wall and considered whether the whole thing wasn't just a dream. The wall light was burning right over my head. Everything around me was taking on a new appearance. The window curtain, the television set, and the outline of the shadows had all become portents of something inscrutable. Everything was becoming dependent on me, subject to my will. I decided to eliminate the wardrobe cabinet. Its lacquer finish suddenly turned dull, the outline of the door became blurred, the rear wall burst open, and an unshapely black hole was soon crawling with writhing, slithering shapes. I tried to restore the cabinet but couldn't. The center of the room was gradually being enveloped by the shadows in the corners. I could only rescue those objects that still remained in the light. I reached for the phone; the receiver, which had taken on a perverse and mocking shape, slipped out of my hand. The telephone became a gray rock with a rough surface, the dial a hole. My fingers penetrated the surface and touched something cold. There was a ball-point pen lying on the table. Exerting all my powers of concentration to keep the pen from disappearing, I scrawled a message across the telegram in large letters:

11:00   NAUSEA
11:50   ILLUSIONS AND DELUSIONS

But while I was writing I lost all control over my surroundings and at any moment I expected the room to collapse. Then the unexpected happened: I noticed something was going on in my immediate vicinity. I realized that the immediate vicinity was my own body. It was stretching; my hands and feet were moving farther away from me. Afraid that I might bang my head against the ceiling, I made a dive for the bed. I lay on my back but had trouble breathing; my chest swelled like the dome of Saint Peter's; my hands became big enough to scoop up several pieces of furniture, if not the whole room. A nightmare, I told myself. Just ignore it! By then I had stretched so far my extremities were dissolving into darkness. They were so distant from me that I'd lost all sensation in them. Only my interior was left. A vast and labyrinthine region, a gulf lying between my mind and the world, which in fact had ceased to exist. I leaned out breathlessly over my own abyss. Where I once had had a pair of lungs, intestines, and veins, I now saw only thoughts—gigantic thoughts; and in those thoughts, my life, my tangled and splintered life, as it glowed, turned to charcoal and finally into ashes. I watched it disintegrate into a fiery dust, a black Sahara. The black Sahara was my life. The room in which I was lying like a fish on the ocean floor had shrunk to the size of a grain of sand; it, too, was a part of me. The more I kept expanding beyond the limits of my body, the more terrified I became. Little by little I was being consumed by an awesome power, by the power of my expanding mass, which was devouring everything in a greedy surge. I groaned in despair as I found myself sucked into the depths; I tried raising myself up by supporting my elbows on the mattress, now located somewhere in the middle of the earth. I was afraid that with one jerk of my hand I might cave in the walls. It can't be, I kept telling myself, but I could feel it in every nerve and fiber of my body. In a senseless attempt to escape, I crawled out of bed, got down on my knees, and groped along the wall for the light switch. The room was inundated by a razor-sharp whiteness. I saw the table oozing with an iridescent film; the telephone bleached bone-white; and in the mirror my own face glistening with sweat. I recognized the face, but nothing else had changed. I tried to understand what was happening to me, to get at the force that was bursting to get out. Was I that force? I was and I wasn't. My swollen hand was still mine. But what if it turned into a mountain of flesh and tried to crush me with its seething, bubbling mass? Could I then still claim it as my own and not the force expanding it? Whenever I tried to resist the metamorphosis, I was too late; by then the change had already taken place. With a mere glance I could remove the ceiling; under my gaze everything buckled, caved in, collapsed—melted like a house of wax on fire. You're hallucinating! I kept telling myself, and the words would bounce back like an echo from a well. I shoved myself away from the wall, spread out my feet, watched as they kept sinking into the mushy parquet flooring, turned my head like the dome of some lofty cathedral, and spotted my watch lying on the night stand. The dial was the bottom of a luminous crater; the second hand was ticking off the seconds in eerie slow motion, leaving behind it a trail more white than the dial's enamel finish, while the dial expanded to become a battlefield traversed by military columns. The chalky ground between the marching ranks was ripped apart by explosions, the smoke assumed the shape of faces—malleable masks of mute agony. Swarms of antlike soldiers congealed into a vitreous mass; their blood ran out to form round pools of red mud, but they marched on, dust-covered and bloodied, to the steady accompaniment of a drum roll. The battle gradually diminished in scale as I put down the watch, but never ceased. Suddenly the room became tilted, began rotating in slow motion, and hurled me toward the ceiling. Something broke my fall. I dropped down on my hands and knees and lay by the bed as the room gradually came to a stop and everything settled back into place. Stretched out with my head on the floor like a dog, I glanced up at the watch leaning against the lamp on the night stand; it was a quarter to one.

All was quiet again; the second hand crept along like an ant. I sat up on the floor and was braced by its coolness. In the austere light the room assumed the appearance of a solid crystal filled with a faint ringing and a blinding refulgence. In this atmosphere of extreme clarity the furniture, the folds in the window curtain, the shadows cast by the table stood out with unspeakable perfection. I paid little attention to the beauty of my surroundings; I was like an off-duty fireman who, continually on the lookout for smoke in a theater auditorium, is oblivious of the beauty on stage. I stood up, feeling woozy, and, overcoming the estrangement in my fingers, scribbled a few more notes on the telegram:

12:50   RELIEF
PLIMASINE IN THE MORNING
ORLY—BARBERSHOP

More I didn't know. While I was bent over the table I felt another change coming on. The reflection on the table top began fluttering like dragonfly wings; then the whole table rose up and flapped its gray-ribbed bat wings in my face till it completely shrouded the milky glow of the night light. The edge of the table turned limp as soon as I grabbed it with my hands. I could neither escape this rush of transformations nor catch up with it—they were becoming more accelerated now, more monstrous, more majestic, more mocking—they passed through me like a breeze—I closed my eyelids—I didn't need eyes to see them. I recall making a vague but determined effort to expel the foreign element, to puke it out; it was no use. I tried to defend myself as best I could; I was becoming less a spectator and more a part of these teeming visions—their quivering, shuddering flaw.

Some time after one o'clock I managed to surface again. It came in waves now, like the process of peristalsis; at each stage it promised to be over, only to become more intense during the sequel. The visions began to let up between two and three, which proved to be even worse than before because now everything assumed its normal appearance again, only this time on a different level of consciousness. How to describe it? The furniture and walls became petrified in the middle of some horrible transition; time came to a halt, leaving only the surrounding world, which suddenly stopped advancing toward me like an avalanche and became frozen in a prolonged flash of magnesium. The whole room was like a gasp between two successive screams; its intended target was manifested with undisguised malice in the intricacies of the wallpaper design, in the picture of the Loire castle hanging above the bed, and in the castle's green lawns. This greenery was my sentence; I stared up at it from a kneeling position and realized that I had to lose. Then I began attacking the room—yes, the room; I ripped the cords off the curtains and blinds, yanked the drapes down from their hooks, pulled off the bedcovers, and threw the whole lethal pile into the bathtub. Then I shut the bathroom door and broke the key while trying to jam it into the door's outerlock. Out of breath, I leaned against the doorframe and surveyed the battlefield. I realized it was all a waste of time: it was impossible to remove the windows and walls. I dumped the contents of my bags out onto the floor and dug my way through to the flat metal rings connected by a short rod; Randy had given them to me back in Naples so I could handcuff the murderer when the time came. Now I had him. A bunch of tiny dark objects spilled out from between my shirts—almonds that had fallen out of the package —but I didn't have time to record them, I was afraid I wouldn't make it; so I threw a handful on top of the telegram, pulled an armchair up to the radiator, made myself comfortable in it, and leaned my back against the upholstery; then I pressed my feet down on the floor, handcuffed myself to the radiator pipe, and in a state of unbelievable tension waited for IT to happen, as in the moments before a takeoff. I was propelled neither upward nor downward, however, but inward, into a hot and reddish fog, surrounded by whirling walls, shackled and chained. Straining like a dog on a leash, I could reach only as far as one of the bedposts. I pulled the bed toward me, buried my face in the mattress as if trying to smother a fire, chewed my way through to the foam rubber; but it was too porous to suffocate me, so I grabbed my windpipe with my free hand and squeezed it with all my might. Despair: I still couldn't kill myself. Just before losing consciousness, I remember hearing explosions in my head: I must have banged it against the pipes. I also recall experiencing one final, faint glimmer of hope that this time I would bring it off. Then nothing; I died, and I didn't even find anything strange about the fact that I was conscious of dying. Later I had the sensation of swimming through black waterfalls of unknown grottoes, where the water's roar was so loud it was as if only my sense of hearing had survived. I could hear bells chiming. The black color turned pink. I opened my eyes and beheld a large, strange, pale, and incredibly calm face bent over me. The face belonged to Dr. Barth. I recognized him at once and was about to tell him something to that effect when I suddenly fainted in a most jejune manner.

They found me around four in the morning, handcuffed to the radiator, after some Italians next door had alerted the hotel staff. Since it gave the appearance of being an attack of frenzy, I was given a tranquilizing shot before being rushed to the hospital. After learning of the flight cancellation the following day, Barth had telephoned Orly, been told what had happened to me, and driven straight to the hospital, where I was still lying unconscious. It was thirty hours before I finally regained consciousness. I wound up with several broken ribs, a lacerated tongue, a head full of stitches, and a badly swollen wrist caused by my chafing on the handcuffs. Luckily the radiator to which I had been handcuffed was made of cast iron; one made of synthetic material would have broken, and I would have jumped out the window.

$$* \quad * \quad *$$

A Canadian biologist has proved that people resistant to balding have the same nucleic acid in their skin tissue as catarrhine monkeys, which are also immune to balding. This substance, which goes by the name of "monkey's hormone," has been proved effective in the treatment of baldness. In Europe, the manufacture of a hormone ointment was begun three years ago by a Swiss company operating under license from the American firm of Pfizer. The Swiss succeeded in modifying the hormone's chemical structure in a way that made it more effective but also more sensitive to heat, a factor resulting in its rapid degradation.

When the skin is exposed to the sun, the hormone undergoes a chemical alteration; if it is then combined with Ritalin it can be converted into Dr. Dunant's compound X, a depressant, though only when administered in large doses does it produce any toxic effects. Ritalin is present in the blood stream of those who use it, while the hormone is applied topically in the form of an ointment that contains the added ingredient hyaluronidase to enable the medication to be absorbed through the skin and to enter the circulation. But in order to produce a psychotropic reaction, one would have to apply at least two hundred grams of the ointment daily and exceed the recommended dosage of Ritalin.

Certain compounds, such as cyanide plus sulfur—or thiocyanates—act as catalysts that can increase the psychotropic toxicity a million times. The chemical symbols—CNS—provide the key to the riddle. Cyanide is one of the chemical constituents of bitter almonds; it is what gives them their distinctively bitter and pungent taste. Some time ago a number of almond factories in Naples became infested with cockroaches. The disinfectant used to exterminate them contained sulfur, traces of which found their way into the emulsion used to coat the almonds before they were placed in the oven. As long as the oven temperature remained low, nothing happened; but as soon as the temperature rose high enough to allow the sugar to caramelize, the cyanide combined with the sulfur to form cyanogen sulfide, or a thiocyanate. But when introduced into the body by itself, cyanogen sulfide is incapable of having a catalytic effect on factor X; ionic sulfur must also be present in the reacting bodies. Ions in the form of sulfates and sulfites were traced back to the mineral baths. Therefore, a person would die if he used the hormone ointment, took Ritalin and mineral baths, and ate the Neapolitan-style sugar-roasted almonds. The catalytic reaction triggered by the thiocyanates involved such negligible amounts as to be undetectable except by chromatography. A prerequisite for involuntary self-destruction was a fondness for sweets. Those who couldn't eat sweets because of diabetes, or who weren't partial to sweets, escaped unharmed. The Swiss version of the ointment had been available on the European market for two years, which explained why no cases had been reported before that. No cases were reported in the States, because the only product available there was Pfizer's, which was not nearly so sensitive to heat as the European variety. And since the product was intended exclusively for men, it was only natural that women were not included among the victims.

Proque also fell into the trap, but by a different route. Though he had never had any need of the scalp ointment, gone to the beach, or taken mineral baths, the sulfur ions entered his circulation through inhalation of sulfur dioxide from hypo used in developing photos; the Ritalin came from the stimulant prescribed for his lethargy; and the compound X, from Dr. Dunant's glasses. All the time the learned and patient doctor was busy running tests on every scrap, every speck of dust inside Proque's shop, taking specimens of the plywood partition and the grinding powder, little did he realize that the mystery substance was located approximately four meters above his head—in a bag of sugar-coated almonds lying at the bottom of a dresser drawer.

What had alerted Barth's chemists and provided them with the missing link were the almonds found with my notes on the table.

One incidental though rather amusing detail: after my return to the States, I was told by a chemist friend of mine that the flowers of sulfur sprinkled in my bed by little Pierre could not have acted as a chemical agent, for the reason that elemental sulfur, obtained as a solid through sublimation, is monionic and insoluble in water. My friend came up with the hypothesis that the ionic sulfur found in my blood must have come from wine that had been allowed to sulfurize. Following the French custom, I was in the habit of drinking wine with every meal; this last time, however, I had drunk exclusively at Barth's place, since I never ate any meals out. The chemists from the CNRS must have been aware of this but preferred not to embarrass their boss by insinuating he was serving his guests bad wine.

I was later asked whether the almonds had been my great discovery. Nothing would have been easier than to give a yes or no answer, but the truth was I didn't know. During my rampage, when I'd gone around destroying everything within reach, dumping everything that seemed lethal into the bathtub, I had certainly acted like a madman, but in this madness of mine there was an element of self-preservation. It might have been similar with the almonds. I'd wanted to make a note of them, that much I know, though this reflex of mine could have been the result of many years of practice. I had been trained to record things under conditions of maximum stress, to assess the relevance of something regardless of my own personal opinion. It might have been just a flash of intuition that led me to connect the thunderstorm, my sneezing fit, the pill stuck in my throat, the almonds, and the image of Proque making that last trip into the corner candy store on Rue Amélie. But that strikes me as too good to be true. I might have associated the almonds with the Naples affair at the sight of the miniature Vesuvius displayed in the shopwindow. Though not directly related to the case, Vesuvius turned out to be the magic link that put me on the right trail. Though if you look back carefully over my report, you will see there were many times during the investigation when I thought I was on the right trail, and yet nothing came of it. Barth was on the right track, too, though he was wrong in suspecting a political motive. He was right in questioning the method of selection—the "group of eleven"—and also in saying the victims included only unmarried foreigners because the latter were more apt to be isolated from their Italian surroundings by their unfamiliarity with the language and the absence of any dependents. The first sign of a toxic reaction was always a change in disposition, which only someone close to the victim would have been able to detect in the early stages. Subsequent investigation revealed several "abortive cases" involving Italians and foreigners who had come to Naples with their wives. In every case the pattern was identical: alarmed by her husband's erratic behavior, the wife would start to keep a closer eye on him, and the moment he started having hallucinations she would do her utmost to persuade him to leave the country. This impulse to return home was an instinctive reaction in the face of an unknown danger. The Italians, on the other hand, would immediately be put under a psychiatrist's care—usually under family pressure—at which time they would be advised to stop driving, to discontinue the Plimasine, and to interrupt their bathing treatment; as a result of this abrupt change, the symptoms would rapidly disappear. A chance circumstance kept the investigation from uncovering these "abortive cases" earlier. In each and every instance someone from the victim's immediate family would come to claim the prepaid subscription, but since the books of the various spas recorded only the financial transactions, and not the reason for the cancellation, there was absolutely no way the persons in question could be traced.

There were a number of other factors impeding the investigation. No one likes to brag about using an ointment as a preventive against baldness. Those who made no fuss about going bald, or who preferred wearing a wig to using an ointment, escaped unharmed, though there was no way investigators could know this at the time. Those who avoided the hormone had no reason to testify, since they were safe and sound, while those who did use it died. No packages containing the Swiss ointment were ever found among the victims' personal belongings because the medication was supposed to be kept stored in the refrigerator. This was easy enough to do at home, but not in a hotel, so rather than take the medication along with them on their travels, the more conscientious among the older men would rely on the local barbers. The directions called for one application every ten days, which meant that only one application was needed during the time spent in Naples. And of course during the investigation it never occurred to anyone to canvass the local barbershops to find out what they were rubbing into the scalps of certain customers.

And lastly, just as all the victims shared a definite physical resemblance, so, too, they all had certain psychological traits in common. All were men well past their prime, still very conscious of their appearance, struggling with old age but reluctant to admit it. Those men who were already in their sixties and completely bald had given up trying to look younger than their age and had stopped shopping around for miraculous cures, whereas those who were thirty and had grown prematurely bald were not likely to require any bathing treatment for advanced rheumatism. Therefore the ones who were exposed to the greatest danger were those who had already crossed the shadow line. In retrospect, the more closely one examined the facts, the more interrelated they became. For example, the chemical poisonings all took place during the blooming season, when drivers were more apt to use Plimasine, and since patients with acute asthma were physically unable to drive, they would have had no need for a drug intended for drivers.

Barth was gracious enough to keep me company during my stay in the hospital, so I decided to pay him a farewell visit before flying back to the States. Pierre was keeping a lookout by the stairs but ducked out of sight the moment he saw me coming. I knew what was on his mind and promised him I wouldn't forget about his helmet. Barth had another visitor, Dr. Saussure, now wearing a shirt with frilled cuffs instead of a frock coat, with a pocket watch dangling from his neck instead of a calculator. While he browsed through some books in the library, Barth spoke to me about one of the supreme ironies of the case: even though it had been inoperative and unprogrammed the whole time, the computer had proved enormously beneficial to the investigation. Because if I hadn't flown to Paris with the idea of using the computer, I never would have stayed at Barth's place, never would have aroused the sympathy of his grandmother, and little Pierre never would have come to my rescue with the flowers of sulfur after my fall on the stairs. . . . In short, the computer played an undisputed role in unraveling the mystery, though in a purely abstract sort of way. With a laugh I commented that the whole combination of fortuitous events leading up to the solving of the mystery now seemed to me more amazing than the mystery itself.

"Now you're committing the egocentrist fallacy!" Saussure exclaimed as he turned around to face us from the bookcase. "This series of yours is not as much a sign of the times as a portent of tomorrow. A vague premonition of things to come. . . ."

"Do you understand it?"

"I see only the warning signs. Mankind has multiplied to such an extent that it's now starting to be governed by atomic laws. The movement of gas atoms is chaotic, but out of this

- 176 -

chaos are born such things as stable pressure, temperature, specific gravity, and so on. Your accidental success looks like a long series of extraordinary coincidences. But it only *seems* that way to you. You will probably argue that besides your falling down Barth's stairs and accidentally inhaling sulfur, a number of other factors were necessary to trigger the chain reaction: your scouting trip to Rue Amélie, your sneezing fit, the decision to buy some almonds for your nephews, the flight cancellation, the crowded hotel, the barber, and even the fact that the barber was a Gascon. . . ."

"Oh, why stop there," I intruded. "If I hadn't broken my tail bone in the liberation of France, I wouldn't have had a relapse on the ecalator in Rome, or here, either, for that matter. And if I hadn't wound up in front of the assassin on the escalator, my picture wouldn't have landed on the cover of *Paris-Match*. And if it hadn't been for the picture, I would have spent the night in Paris instead of fighting for a room at the Hotel Air France, and that would have been the end of it. The chances of my being there at all during the explosion were astronomically small. I could have booked another flight; I could have been standing on another step. . . . Not to mention all the other astronomical improbabilities that came before and after! For instance, if I hadn't heard about the Proque affair, I wouldn't have decided to fly back to Rome just when the flights were being canceled . . . and in a way that was the purest coincidence of all."

"You mean your finding out about the Proque affair? I don't believe it was a coincidence. The doctor and I were just talking about it before you came in. You were briefed because of the political infighting going on between Sûreté and Défense. Someone was out to discredit a certain military official who was playing politics to promote Dr. Dunant. You were caught in a billiard game."

"Was I supposed to be a ball or a cue?"

"Our guess is that they were using you to get the Proque case reopened so they could damage Dunant's reputation. . . ."

"But I still don't see what my coming to Paris had to do with all this political infighting."

"It had absolutely nothing to do with it. That's why the large number of coincidences strikes you as being contrary to common sense. But I say to hell with common sense! By itself each segment of your experience is plausible enough, but the trajectory resulting from the aggregate of these segments borders on being a miracle. That's what you thought, wasn't it?"

"Yes."

"But meanwhile the very thing I was telling you about three weeks ago has happened. Imagine a firing range where a postage stamp is set up as a target a half mile away. Let's make it a ten-centime stamp, with a picture of Marianne on it. Along comes a fly and leaves a speck the size of a dot. Now let several sharpshooters start firing away at the dot. They will surely miss it, because at that distance they won't even be able to see it. But now suppose a hundred mediocre marksmen were to start firing for weeks on end. You can bet that one of their bullets will eventually hit its target. Not because the man who fired it was a phenomenal marksman, but because of the sheer density of fire. Wouldn't you agree?"

"Yes, but that still doesn't explain—"

"Wait, I'm not finished yet. It's summer now, and the range is crawling with flies. The probability of hitting the dot was extremely small. But the probability of simultaneously hitting both the dot and a fly that happens to wander into the bullet's path is even smaller. The probability of hitting the dot and *three* flies with the same bullet would be—to use your words—astronomically small. And yet I assure you that such a coincidence would come to pass as long as the firing was kept up long enough."

"Excuse me, but you're talking about a whole barrage, while I was just one of a series. . . ."

"That's an illusion. At the precise moment the bullet hits both the dot and the three flies, then it, too, is only one of a series. The lucky marksman will be just as amazed as you were, even though there would be nothing so terribly miraculous or unusual about the fact that *he* hit it, because, you see, *somebody would have had to hit it*. See what I mean? Common sense isn't worth a damn here. My prediction came true. The Naples mystery was the result of a random causality, and it was the same random causality that solved it. The law of probability applies to both members of the proposition. Needless to say, if only one of the set of necessary conditions had gone unfulfilled, you never would have been drugged, but sooner or later someone would have met all the conditions. One, three, five years from now. And that is so because we now live in such a dense world of random chance, in a molecular and chaotic gas whose 'improbabilities' are amazing only to the individual human atoms. It's a world where yesterday's rarity becomes todays cliché, and where today's exception becomes tomorrow's rule."

"O.K., but I was the one—"

He didn't let me finish. Barth, who knew Saussure, looked at both of us with twinkling eyes, as if trying his best not to laugh.

"Excuse me, but if it hadn't been you, it would have been someone else."

"Who? Some other detective?"

"I don't know and I don't care. Someone, that's all. By the way, is it true you're planning to write a book about the case?"

"As a matter of fact, I am. I even have a publisher ... but why do you ask?"

"Because that's also related. Just as some bullet is bound to hit its target, someone was bound to crack the case. And if that's so, then regardless of the publisher or author, the publication of this book was also a mathematical certainty."

November 1975

STANISLAW LEM

Tales of Pirx the Pilot

How Pirx made the grade as a space pilot is probably even a mystery to him.

His first solo flight as a clumsy cadet is further complicated by the antics of two stowaway flies. Then a routine mission to the moon only returns to earth because of his instinctive mistrust of technology. Even as an off-duty passenger he characteristically refrains from minding his own business when a transgalactic liner receives a distress call. And when he commands the ageing revamp of a notorious wreck the ship gives up some of its ghostly secrets.

With Pirx, Stanislaw Lem has created a uniquely fallible human being to explore and challenge the intricate world of science.

'Lem outdistances nearly all the most popular startrekkers' *Time*

'In the Pirx tales it is the adventure story Lem puts to use and he handles it with the ease of Jack London' *San Francisco Chronicle*

'Lem has no equal in his literary explorations of machines and their physical and philosophical potentialities' *New York Times*

STANISLAW LEM

His Master's Voice

Something completely escapes the notice of the
majority of eager young scientists studying the
fashionable new phenomenon of neutrino radiation. The cosmic emission from the darkness of
the stars is conveying a message for humanity.

His Master's Voice becomes the name for the
highly secret project to decode the Sender's alien
message. But as the scientists collude and quarrel
in the race to discover whether the message is a
gift or a weapon they find their world, and all its
points of reference, turned bewilderingly upon its
head.

'A rarified treat'   *The Times*

'A mixture of hilarious pseudo-science and pro-
found, gloomy, witty reflections on the limitations
of twentieth century man . . .'   *The Scotsman*

'By the last chapters one is racing like a romance
novel addict'   *New York Times*

STANISLAW LEM

Return from the Stars

Over 1 million copies sold.

A ten-year expedition to the stars returns astronaut Hal Bregg to an earth he barely recognises. For ten of his years amount to a hundred and twenty-seven in elapsed earth time.

Once the pioneer of his own generation, Bregg now feels like a Neanderthal man. Civilisation has gone soft; medically denatured in early childhood, pampered by robots, entertained with illusions and entirely unconcerned with the worlds of learning or beyond, human beings idly pursue youth, ease and trivialities. So when Bregg falls passionately but inexpertly for a young woman who understands as little about his world as he does about hers, he is faced with a uniquely bewildering choice . . .

Return from the Stars is an engrossing and comically surreal novel that asks some of Lem's favourite questions about the strange impulses that propel humanity.

'One of the most intelligent, erudite and comic writers working today' *Anthony Burgess*

'Stanislaw Lem is the premier science-fiction writer alive' *New York Times*

C. J. CHERRYH

The Paladin

Beyond the haunted hills of Mon lives Shoka, Lord Saukendar, the paragon swordmaster who escaped the corrupt court of Chiyaden for a reclusive life of peace. The veteran master turns away all the hopeful youths who risk their lives to seek his mountain exile and learn his secrets.

But it is the girl named Taizu, disguising herself as a scarred and half-starved urchin, who secures the promise of his tutelage and surpasses all the swordsmen he has crossed.

With the Emperor approaching his thirtieth year, Chiyaden's court is still governed by the implacable Lord Ghita while its provinces are overrun by marauding bands of mercenaries and bandits. Only Taizu's passion for justice and revenge can persuade the legendary Lord Saukendar to join her in taking up his sword once more to restore the Throne of Chiyaden to its rightful heir.

'Read *The Paladin* and you'll never settle for another ordinary sword-wielding female'. *Locus*

A Selected List of Science Fiction Available from Mandarin

☐	7493 0021 3	**Kinsman**	Ben Bova	£3.50
☐	7493 0083 8	**Millennium**	Ben Bova	£3.50
☐	7493 0120 1	**Peacekeepers**	Ben Bova	£3.50
☐	7493 0105 8	**The Compleat Traveller in Black**	John Brunner	£3.50
☐	7493 0007 8	**The Chronicles of Morgaine**	C. J. Cherryh	£4.99
☐	7493 0154 6	**Downbelow Station**	C. J. Cherryh	£3.99
☐	7493 0006 X	**Exile's Gate**	C. J. Cherryh	£3.99
☐	7493 0068 X	**Pride of Chanur**	C. J. Cherryh	£2.99
☐	7493 0100 7	**Serpents Reach**	C. J. Cherryh	£3.50
☐	7493 0038 8	**Highway of Eternity**	Clifford D. Simak	£2.99
☐	7493 0099 X	**Off-Planet**	Clifford D. Simak	£3.50
☐	7493 0079 5	**Where the Evil Dwells**	Clifford D. Simak	£3.50
☐	7493 0103 1	**Deep Space**	Eric Frank Russell	£2.99
☐	7493 0047 7	**A Splendid Chaos**	John Shirley	£3.99
☐	7493 0037 X	**Ravenmoon**	Peter Tremayne	£3.50